THE CAILIN

by

Lois S. Williams, Ph.D.

Kevin Ann Planchet, collaborator

Williams, Lois S., Ph.D.

The Cailin

ISBN 978-0-6151-9986-3

First edition

Dedication

"This book is dedicated to my phenomenal and supportive husband, Anderson James Williams, Jr., MD and my mother-in-law, the late Bertha B. Williams, who was always wise beyond her years, and my birth children and stepchildren (especially Michele) who are productive citizens all striving to make a difference in a global society."

In addition, this book is dedicated to my precious grandchildren,

Jonathan, Sara, Little Archie and Bruce

I love you all so much!!

Acknowledgments

I would like to acknowledge my husband, Anderson James Williams Jr., M.D. After more than 20 years of marriage, you continue to express unconditional love, patience, and cooperation; you expressed these attributes not only during the writing of this book, but you have also exhibited these qualities throughout our lives together.

I will never forget the lessons taught to me by my mother-in-law, the late Bertha B. Williams – her wit, wisdom, and love inspired this book, in the hopes that it be shared with children around the world. Bertha recited poems from memory and poetry she learned in school and in her travels. I often wished I had recorded those delicate moments because they were indeed unforgettable....moments of "wit 'n wisdom". I find myself re-reading books she held dear. Those same readings have served as an inspiration for her children and grandchildren as they face the challenges in life.

Special appreciation and gratitude to my editor and friend, Kevin Ann Planchet. Kevin Ann is a native of New Orleans and has been writing since she was twelve years old. She is a former television reporter and a mother of three. Her career has segued into management, non-profit work, and literacy training with children. But no matter what she does outside the home, she always goes back to her passion, which is writing. *The Cailin* is her first collaboration. It is hoped that this is just the beginning for many great publications to follow. It was Kevin Ann's inner strength that impressed me, and her we-can-do-it attitude that enabled me to complete this publication.

In this publication, I have attempted to share with you, life in a fairy world.

Forward

Sarah Grace Littleton, my step granddaughter, can see fairies. The problem is, she can't really tell anyone. She's already in trouble at school, and the last thing she needs is more. But, a fairy named Fiona is buzzing in her ear, warning of dire consequences if Sarah Grace doesn't develop the power within herself to help save their two worlds.

Sarah Grace's immediate world consists of her family, including her Grammy, who seems to belong in another world, as well. Her best friend, Wendy, is a foster child, who may be taken from her, and her brothers who are a constant source of loving annoyance. It's a lot of work for an eleven year old, but it's up to her to learn how to bring these two worlds together, all the while discovering the incredible child she'll become.

"Cailin" is the Irish word for girl, and seemed a perfect title for this 40,000 word 'tweener' novel, since so much of our fantasy world is routed in Celtic mythology. This novel manuscript was the collaboration of two African-American women, who believed this kind of tale, with a minority character, would appeal, not only to that community, but to others as well.

As you share this reading with your children it is hoped that it will encourage good listening, selective readings that will allow them appreciate the importance of family and family life. To develop good character traits and values such as humility, honesty, responsibility, dependability, perseverance and the ability to dream big dreams about the many possibilities in life, to become whatever they want to become. Further, it is hoped this book will help the readers to exercise good judgment regarding decisions that influence their lives.

THE CAILIN

Introduction

Hierarchy of the Fae World

Queen Nivia

Supreme Being of the Fairy World, Queen Nivia is an immortal and will rule until she chooses to step down. Her power is absolute. Queen Nivia works with the beings from other worlds to insure the proper balance between the mystical and the practical; the fairy and the human. In appearance, she is an ethereal yellow light, with a transparent human form, and delicate wings.

Fairies

Fairies are also immortals, who serve at the pleasure of the Queen. While similar in appearance, the addition of color to their beings and more human-like features distinguishes them from the Queen. There are sixteen levels of the fairy realm, and true responsibility for the world around them doesn't begin until they've reached their two thousandth year. All fairies are responsible for the education of their human child, for they are the link between their two worlds. One cannot survive without the other.

Guardians

While Fairies are teachers and have contact with their human for a specific amount of time, guardians are meant to be a constant, but invisible force in the child's life. Children who can see fairies are not immortals, and are therefore vulnerable to threats from each world. It is the guardian's job to protect the child from evil. The problem with guardians, is that they come from the ranks of children who see fairies, and since they are human, they too are vulnerable to physical threats, as well as human frailties like love, anger, jealousy, and deception.

Grogochs

Grogochs are basically the domestics of the fairy world. They serve many purposes, most of are determined on a daily basis by the Queen herself. Some are Earthers, who spend their days digging for whatever they can find. Some are Gatekeepers, who protect the entrance of the Fae World. Others simply gather food and other necessities for the fairies. Though they may live for thousands of years, they are not immortals, and in the end will disintegrate into some form of nature, such as a rock or dirt.

Enemies

The main enemy of the fairy world is the Droch (droke). Though fairy-like in appearance, their eyes are red and their wings have severe points which are used as weapons. They hate the cold, are affected by nature and the elements, and are unable to disappear. However, they have limited abilities to change shape and size. Extremely strong physically, their real talents lie in their ability to affect the minds of their victims.

Drochs work for the domination of the fairy world and hit at its weakest links---the guardians. If a Droch can poison the mission of a guardian, it can get at a child and disrupt the link between the human and fairy worlds. Drochs are so deceptive that often the guardians don't know they've been infiltrated until it's too late, and the essence of the child has been contaminated. Drochs are sometimes hard to identify, because they take on human form and blend seamlessly into the natural order of things. Queen Nivia is the only immortal being who can destroy a Droch. A human child is the only mortal being who can.

Changelings

A secondary enemy to the Fae World is the changeling, named so because they can take the form of any living thing, be it human, plant or animal. They are a secondary enemy because they are mercenaries, working for whoever will pay them. They work for jewels and precious gemstones. Changelings are not immortals, and they have no conscience. They will work for the Queen just as quickly as they will work for the Drochs. Pure and simple, they offer a service, for which they are paid.

Prologue

Branduff, the Black Raven, considered his next move. This undertaking had not gone well. He'd underestimated the frailty of human beings and was now faced with a dilemma he had not foreseen. The man was dead.

Branduff shivered and stepped away from the body. He could feel the human's blood going cold; see the pink leaving his skin to be replaced with a blue ashen pallor. They have no strength, he thought to himself, but how could they? He shivered inside his mortal coil. Branduff stepped back, took a cleansing breath and closed his eyes. The shell of his human costume melted away. The masculine suit dissolved over his muscular skeleton and was replaced by a sleek and body hugging black skin. Severe and pointed wings sprouted from his shoulder blades, and the pale brown human eyes were replaced with red. He stretched and felt at home again.

The expansive wings spread out to his sides and almost immediately, Branduff found himself perched atop a bell tower overlooking a Catholic school. He thought this would be a good place to find a child. A child attending a church-run school would surely have to be pure of heart. Branduff had thought this man could help him find one, but in the end he'd been too stupid and Branduff had been too impatient. Now, he would have to start all over again.

The moon was rising and cast a gentle shadow over the school and church grounds. Branduff observed the black robed figures who moved in unison with prayer books in one hand and their devotion to God in the other. But Branduff was no fool. Even in this place meant to teach the beauty of selflessness and humility, he knew he would find someone to bring him the immortality he sought. And with that immortality, would come the keys to the Fae Kingdom.

Chapter 1

"There's been a tear in the fabric of our world."

Fiona watched with little interest from a limb inside the Tree of Promise as Queen Nivia brought the Fae Counsel to order. Nivia could best be described as an entity of bright yellow light with the faintest hint of a human form. Her feet never touched the ground as she floated from one spot to the next. She appeared to be suspended in water as her hair and wings skimmed her body on delicate fingers.

Inside the Tree, there were natural labyrinths of wood and leaf growths. Fairies from the four corners of their mystical world crowded around a small fire lit by natural gemstones. While their appearance mimicked that of the Queen, color tinged their beings; and the fairies could be mistaken for the flowers and plants they so often frequented. "It appears that one of our guardians has betrayed us," the Queen continued. The small chamber erupted in protest and Nivia held up one small hand to silence the assembly. "This is a serious offense and must be dealt with immediately."

While Fiona had great respect for the Queen, she found her a little too serious and long-winded. Fiona grudgingly put in an appearance, lounging on her limb and admiring the new colors that had been added to her wings. The iridescent greens and yellows complemented the cinnamon brown of her heart-shaped face, though she just couldn't decide if she wanted to let her curly hair flow just above her shoulders or pull it up into a bun. Fiona pinched her nose as an unmistakably putrid odor made its way to her limb. It could only be Ronan.

"What's all the noise about?"

"Don't you ever bathe?" Fiona asked irritably. It was just like her to have an acquaintance who understood nothing about bodily hygiene.

"What's the point?" Ronan grumbled, pulling his rotund body onto the limb. "I'm an Earther. I'll only get dirty again." Ronan was a round fellow who fashioned his clothes out of the natural things around him. He wore a coat of wood shavings and his hat was made of moss and small leaves.

Fiona shook her head. She'd rather spend the day mindlessly adorning herself than digging through dirt, rocks and muck looking for.....what? Earthers themselves did not know what they searched for, but the search continued. Not an immortal like herself, Earthers did live for eons but eventually became part of the thing they routed around in all their smelly lives. It was weird to think about, though. One day she would look around and Ronan would disappear into the soil, and knowing Ronan, flowers would not appear on his subterranean grave.

The rumbling from below had ceased. Fiona and Ronan looked down to see what the problem was, when they were met with disapproving stares and the stern expression of the Queen herself. They melted back into the leaves of the tree.

"The two of you might want to hear what I have to say," Queen Nivia said with an arched eyebrow, "since it concerns you and your immediate future."

Fiona and Ronan leaned forward with renewed interest.

"As I was saying, one of our Guardians has betrayed us and must be dealt with. Fiona, it is time you made contact with your cailin."

Fiona gasped. "But Your Highness, I don't know anything about little girls! I'm just not ready," she protested.

"Believe me, Your Highness, she isn't ready," Ronan agreed with a chuckle. Fiona didn't take readily to his assessment and pinched him hard.

"Nonsense, child," the Queen said. "You are in your two thousandth year. It was never intended that you would spend your immortality adorning your wings and buzzing through our world with a Grogoch."

This time, it was Ronan who took exception. He accepted that his kind was on the bottom rung of the fairy world, but insults from the Queen were never welcome. Though not as exalted, Grogochs had a purpose as well. And one day, he'd know what it was.

"If it pleases you," the Queen continued, "you may take Ronan with you."

Ronan would have protested at that point, but he'd lost the ability to speak upon hearing the Queen's directive.

"But Your Highness," Fiona continued.....

"You'll leave immediately," Queen Nivia commanded. "And remember, Fiona, you have only until the moonrise of the Summer Solstice to complete your task. If you fail in this, not only will you jeopardize the world of your cailin, but you may find, you too have no world to call home."

"If you'd just been quiet, maybe she wouldn't have even noticed me," Fiona huffed as they made their way out of the tree.

"Don't get mad at me," Ronan spat. "It's not like she picked you out of nowhere. You've been avoiding your cailin duties for eons. The Queen picked you for a reason, so you might as well just get it over with. Anyway, you only have charge of one cailin. Once she's on her way, you ascend to the next level."

Fiona stopped in her tracks and sighed. "That's just it Ronan. I don't know if I know what to do. I wasn't exactly paying attention to everything I was supposed to be learning these last two thousand years."

"Well now's not the time to bring that up," her round friend grumbled. "You'd better figure it out. I don't think you want to go back to the Queen and tell her you don't know what you're doing."

But Fiona was more than a little worried. She wasn't ambitious. There were many levels in the fairy world -- sixteen to be exact. The higher you rose, the more power you achieved. The more power you achieved, the closer you'd be to the Queen's inner circle. That could mean almost unlimited power, though you still served at the pleasure of Nivia. Fiona didn't want that kind of power. It could corrupt. Her one taste of it had been one taste too much. She would avoid that kind of destruction at all costs.

She and Ronan descended into the depths of the Tree of Promise to the tap root which was buried just below the surface. The tap root of a tree gave it life and must always be protected. To that end, Nivia employed several Earthers who served as gatekeepers. They were the first line of defense if ever the tree was threatened.

Prepared to pinch her nose again, Fiona was pleasantly surprised. These Grogochs at the entrance didn't smell at all. She looked at Ronan, query written all over her small face.

"They know their purpose," Ronan explained with an arched eyebrow. "I'm still searching for mine."

"Could you do it with a little less aroma?" she laughed, as they stepped from their hidden home into the sunlight of the Littleton Tree Farm. They were greeted with bright light, dry stagnant air, and dust in their eyes.

"Why in the world would anyone want to live up here?" Ronan asked, shaking his head.

That was just one of many questions running through Fiona's mind. The security of two worlds now depended on a fairy with shaky credentials and a young girl who had no idea that her life would never be the same again.

A sudden gust of wind swept the two of them back to the roots of the tree as a large metal wagon on wheels moved past them.

Sarah Grace pressed her head against the car window as she tried to drown out the sound of her mother scolding her, yet again, for not minding her own business.

"Sarah Grace is a bright student, Mr. and Mrs. Littleton," Sister Sara Ruth had said. "If only she would apply herself to her studies."

Sarah Grace smiled to herself as she reviewed the events of that meeting. She couldn't help but wonder how a woman nicknamed Nosely had such big feet. Sister Sara Ruth always seemed to have difficulty walking and often tripped on her Habit. Apparently, it never occurred to her to have it tailored to fit her properly. She was a tall woman, and thin, to the point of being scrawny. She had a long face with tiny eyes that people rarely saw because she was so busy watching her feet. Sarah Grace laughed to herself.

"You think this is funny young lady?" her dad asked, turning from the driver's seat to look at her.

"No sir," Sarah Grace answered, "I was just thinking."

"Well, if you did that much thinking in school, we wouldn't have to talk so much to your teachers," he said, then winked at her.

Sarah Grace knew that her dad was just going through the motions for her mother's sake. Melvin Littleton knew perfectly well that his daughter was capable of excelling in school, but he also knew that she was a very inquisitive child who was always searching for the answers to a million unasked questions. She was gifted, but bored with the education she was receiving in their small town school. They couldn't afford a private school and a better public school with an accelerated program was too far away.

"Yes, sir," Sarah Grace answered softly, and turned to watch a swirl of dust that seemed to be racing alongside the car. It wasn't a windy day; in fact, it wasn't even a breezy day. It was late September, a sunny, cloudless day and yet; this dust ball seemed to be riding on something peculiar.

Sarah Grace forgot about the dust ball as the car rolled up the long driveway and under the big sign that said "Littleton's Tree Farm". The farm had long ago been used as an actual produce farm, but Mr. Littleton was very pleased to own the largest tree farm in Buncombe County. There were only a few animals left, including her brother Brucie's milk cow, that had at no point offered any milk. There was a family of ducks that Mrs. Littleton insisted had to be there in order to call it "a real farm," and there was Rex, the German Shepherd. Rex was only two years old, but he had found a great friend in Sarah Grace, and watched in grand amusement at all the trouble his friend seemed to find for herself.

Mr. Littleton had taken down most of the buildings and converted the farm into a tree farm on which they grew Christmas trees and a bunch of shrubs and other plants, and trees that didn't interest anyone but her parents. It was the biggest tree farm around. Normally there were people coming and going, trucks hauling this or that in and out, but today was a quiet day much to the comfort of the animals wandering aimlessly through the yard.

"Watch out Mel!" Mrs. Littleton shrieked. "If you hit my ducks…"

"What are you going to do Vel?" Melvin interrupted, "you're going to find a way to make dinner out of them, that's what, and good riddance to them. That'll be one less thing to kick out of my way in the morning." Velvet Littleton knew he would never kick her ducks, but that didn't stop her from tossing him a warning glance before walking into the house. "Oh, I don't have time for this kind of foolishness," she fussed. "I have to check on Grammy."

"I'll do it, Momma. " Sarah Grace ran to her room before her mother could remind her of the chores she was supposed to do as punishment. She wasn't listening in the car and figured she'd corner her dad later and ask him what she said. Sarah Grace did not mean to disregard her mother, but the woman upset easily about everything and half the time, she was just venting her exhaustion from having to deal with the people at the office. She was a travel advisor for a huge business investment company in Raleigh. Velvet managed to stay nervous about something all the time and handed out punishments for the sake of feeling effective. Sarah Grace's oldest brother, Jonathan, was almost sixteen and kept to himself a lot. He was very smart, but more interested in girls than being at home. Her brother Brucie just enjoyed being a pest.

Sarah Grace moved down the wide hall of the sprawling ranch style home to the very last door. It was open, as it always was. It was a pretty room, with lots of ferns and potted flowers. A handmade patchwork quilt hung on the wall above a sturdy four poster bed with goose down mattresses. The room always smelled of peppermint and jasmine, Grammy's favorite fragrances.

"Grammy?" she called.

"YAAA!!!"

Sarah Grace spun around screaming as the closet door flew open.

Grammy jumped out with two feather dusters in her hands. "I gotcha, Bumblebee, I gotcha!!"

Trying to catch her breath, she looked at her 69-years-young grandmother. "Are you crazy?"

"Yes, and you should be warned there's insanity on both sides of your family and it doesn't skip a generation," Madeline Toussaint assured her. She winked and sat down on her bed. "So what'd you do today?"

"It wasn't that big a deal," Sarah Grace threw up her hands and sighed. "That dumb boy was bothering me and Wendy, again," she groaned with emphasis. "I don't know why he's always hanging around us, the little pain in the butt." She threw herself on the bed next to her grandmother and was already getting annoyed as Grammy proceeded to laugh herself silly. "It's not funny. I'm gonna be slave labor for my family for the rest of my life because I punched that boy."

"No slaves from this family," she repeated, as she was likely to, whenever she could squeeze it in. Grammy was very proud of the fact that their ancestors had managed to avoid becoming enslaved. Sarah Grace's maternal ancestors were originally from the African nation of Tanzania, but relocated to the island of Seychelles. Around the turn of the twentieth century the family arrived in the United States. While the racism they'd endured in this country had been extremely difficult, there was something liberating about a past free of slavery. "You punched him!" Grammy exclaimed, properly impressed.

Sarah Grace noticed her Grammy was always impressed when females exerted themselves in even the smallest struggle. In a conversation that always began with, 'When I was a little girl.....' the girl would usually come out the loser. She was brought out of her daydream with a gentle thump to her forehead.

"Maybe he likes you."

Her face immediately screwed up like she'd eaten bad prunes.

"If Devon liked me anymore, he'd push me off a cliff," she laughed, with as much sarcasm as she could muster.

"But that's how boys act. It's how men act sometimes, too. To be honest, your grandfather still gets on my last nerve, even from the grave."

"Has he been talking to you again?" Sarah Grace asked, sure she didn't want to know the answer.

"We're not speaking right now."

"What did he do this time?" she asked, rising off the bed and following Grammy over to her exceptionally feminine vanity. The top was covered with antique atomizers and little jewelry boxes filled with loose gemstones and pins in the shapes of butterflies, fairies and birds. Since Sarah Grace was her only granddaughter, she'd told her on more than one occasion that all of these things would one day be hers. Personally, she found the room a little too pink and fussy.

"Sarah Grace!" her father's voice boomed down the hallway.

Grammy threw her a warning wink. "See ya later."

Sarah Grace groaned. Every conversation she'd ever had with her grandmother ended with an unanswered question, and she suspected Grammy liked it that way. Back in her room, she dropped her books on the dresser and glanced at herself in the mirror. She had more significant problems than a nun berating her abilities of concentration. She never would have been involved in anything if that boy hadn't been bothering her and Wendy.

Wendy had long black hair, which she wore loose, down to her shoulders. Sarah Grace wanted to wear more grown-up styles, but her mother liked to keep her eleven-year-old daughter looking like a two-year-old with pigtails and ribbons. She had those two long plaits down her back every day. Sometimes, she just wished she were prettier, like the girls she saw on television. Her father said she was beautiful, but she didn't like her little button nose and soft brown eyes.

Sarah Grace's thoughts were interrupted as her favorite brother, Brucie, burst into her room and slapped her square on the back.

"Good going, Sis. School's almost over and you're in trouble again. What did you do this time?"

"Shut up Brucie. I wasn't doing anything."

"Then, why are you in trouble?"

"I was late for chapel."

"And?"

"And I smacked Devon, okay?"

"That makes how many times since school started?"

"Not enough, if you ask me!"

"Never mind that, son," Melvin said from the doorway. "Go find something to do and leave your sister alone. She's got work to do."

Sarah Grace looked at her dad, thankful that he could read the lost look on her face. "Laundry little girl, get to it," he said and walked away.

She groaned under her breath and crossed her fingers in hopes that there wasn't much to do. It wasn't even laundry day, it was Thursday. Laundry days were Saturday and Wednesday. Sarah Grace walked down to the basement and turned up her nose as she sorted her brothers' smelly socks and wondered how it was they didn't blow holes in their underwear with the many farting contests they built into each day. How boys could be so disgusting, she didn't know; but she promised herself she would only have girls.

When Sarah Grace woke that sunny Thursday, there was no hint of anything out of the ordinary. She had prepared for the conference with Sister Sara Ruth, and that seemed to be all that the day needed. But, there was something that kept waking her up during the night, like something or someone was trying to communicate with her. A tiny voice was whispering in her ear. Without turning on the light, she could only see that this voice was coming from something that looked like a tiny bird, or maybe it was a bat... whatever it was, it was talking; that is, until she turned into a ball of light and disappeared through the window. There was something about the things around her which seemed confusing and unreal.

Sarah Grace went back up to her room at the end of the hallway and found Rex sniffing her curtains. She stood and watched him for a moment to see what he would do next, but he just turned and looked at her, then returned to his sniffing. He turned one more time as if to ask if she was just going to stand there, or join him. Sarah Grace understood her dog and walked slowly to the window. She could just make out what appeared to be tiny wings sticking out from the curtain, which was wrapped around the tiny shape. The closer Sarah Grace got, the more she could see this thing was shivering and shaking the whole curtain.

Sarah Grace slowly turned back the curtain and was astonished to see a tiny woman, about four inches tall standing on the windowsill with her face in her hands, shaking like a leaf. Sarah Grace read about this in books, but she never dreamed that she would meet a real live fairy.

Sarah Grace looked over her shoulder to see if anyone was behind her, particularly Brucie, who was fond of sneaking up on her. When she turned back to the window, the fairy was gone. Had she just imagined it? What was she thinking? Maybe it was her overactive imagination getting away from her again. No. There was certainly something there. Even Rex knew, but he had already found something else to sniff in the room. Sarah Grace shook the thoughts of fairies out of her head and busied herself with studying for her spelling test.

But, sitting at the small desk in her room, vocabulary words were pushed out of her head by something else. As she sat in front of her spelling book, she was bothered by a strange odor. She had just finished the laundry, so it couldn't be dirty clothes in her room, or in the hall, where her brothers usually tossed their dirty things before they made it to the chute. But the odor was that of BO, something she and her friend Wendy detected on one of the nuns at school, and joked about often.

Sarah Grace tapped her pencil on her desk and looked around, trying to find the source of the smell, but didn't see anything, or anyone. She convinced herself that she was imagining things once again and went back to studying until her mother called for dinner.

Sarah Grace sat quietly eating that night, which was unusual. Normally, she would engage her brothers in a battle of wits or whisper secrets to Grammy, just for the sake of annoying her mother.

"Baby, you're awfully quiet. Is there something wrong?" Velvet asked.

"No ma'am, I was just thinking, that's all."

"Thinking what, Sis; about Sister Ruth's big feet?" Both Brucie and Jonathan laughed at the thought. They had seen Sister Nosely's feet during their classes with her and found no less humor in the remembrance now. Even Mr. Littleton joined them briefly in their amusement, as he too had noticed something not quite right about the nun.

"Has anyone noticed anything weird going on today?" Sarah Grace asked. "I mean, things like leaves blowing when the wind isn't, or stuff moving out of place?" Her brothers roared with laughter as they looked at their sister sitting very seriously on the opposite side of the table.

"Maybe it was a fairy," Grammy told her, dropping a silver spoon into her tea. "Now's the season for fairies."

"Mother, really," Velvet scolded.

"Oh Velvet," Grammy scolded right back, "You've always been so snooty. Try as I might, I could never knock it out of you."

"Sis, you have got to get out from behind all those books you read," Jonathan jabbed. "You make it sound like something is haunted."

"Well, how do you know this farm isn't haunted? Where did all the animals go, and why would someone leave just one fat cow in the barn?"

"Hey, you leave Big Mamma alone!" Brucie scolded.

"Never mind," Sarah Grace sighed. "I must be imagining things." Mr. and Mrs. Littleton both looked at their daughter with worried frowns ,and wondered if the tongue lashing she got from her mother on the way home from school was getting to her.

She was a thousand miles away from the car ride home as she

finished her dinner in silence. How wonderful it would be to have her very own fairy! Wendy would be jealous for sure.

Sarah Grace excused herself and went back to her room. She laid out clothes for the next day, then sat at her desk and pulled a book from her growing library.

The book was good, and she was completely immersed, when she got that feeling again. She glanced at the purple clock on the wall, thankful now that it glowed in the dark. It was 8:30 and too dark to see anything clearly. It was a bad habit she had. She adjusted her eyes to the light available, as opposed to adding artificial light, reading as the sun went down. She felt something fly past her face and clip her nose with something soft and velvety that made her sneeze.

Chapter 2

"Oof!" "Ow!"

"What? Who's there?" Sarah Grace asked sleepily, as she switched on the lamp on her desk. Just as the light came on, she could see a tiny body with wings sliding down the wall onto the floor. Thoroughly intrigued now, she peeked under the desk, hoping with her fingers crossed, that she wasn't dreaming this time.

"Well, what are you looking at? Help a girl up, will you?"

"Are you a real fairy?" Sarah Grace asked, trying to hide her excitement.

"Of course, I'm as real as you. Now hold out your hand and help me to the desk. That last sneeze of yours bent one of my wings and I can't jump that high." Sarah Grace held out her hand for the fairy and gently raised her to the desktop. She didn't know whether to laugh or pinch herself to see if she really was awake.

"My name's Fiona, by the way."

"I'm, Sarah…."

"I know who you are Sarah Grace Littleton. I've always

known," Fiona grumbled.

"Really? " She asked, a little bewildered. "Well, it's very nice to meet you, but what are you doing here? I'm not allowed to have people in my room without my parents' permission."

"Oh, don't worry about your parents. They can't see me and for that matter, neither can that mutt of yours that almost ate me earlier."

"But if Rex can't see you, how would he know where to find you and eat you?"

Fiona looked at Sarah Grace and laughed. "Good point SG."

Sarah Grace was so enchanted by the fact that something smaller than her Barbie dolls was walking and talking, she didn't bother to correct her name. Fiona wore her curly brown hair piled on her head, with a silver barrette holding it in place. She wore a silver necklace, silver bracelet, a long green gown the color of a meadow, and red tennis shoes.

"Are you really wearing tennis shoes?" Sarah Grace asked. "I thought all fairies wore little shoes like I put on my Barbies."

"Oh please," Fiona sighed. "Those shoes hurt my feet and as many times as you've sneezed me into a wall, it's easier to run with a more sensible shoe on."

"But you're a fairy. Why don't you just flutter away when I'm about to sneeze?"

"Because I can't always see you. I can't predict the future or your sneezes; so just be careful, okay, SG?"

"Sarah Grace."

"Yeah, yeah."

"So, Miss Fiona, what are you doing here? Are you lost?"

Fiona floated to the stack of books and sat down. "There's no such thing as a 'lost fairy'. I have a reason for being here, but I'm not sure you're going to like it."

Sarah Grace's little nose wrinkled. A fairy was speaking to her, which proved she wasn't crazy. It was the most exciting thing that had ever happened to her. What's not to like about that? Her nose wrinkled again; then she pinched it with two fingers.

Fiona laughed a laugh that sounded like birds singing. "Sorry, that's just Ronan."

"Oh, is that like when humans have gas?"

Fiona nearly laughed herself off the books. "No, silly. Ronan is a Grogoch; what you might consider an elf. Some of them just smell that way because they spend all their time digging in the dirt."

"Why?"

"If I knew the answer to that, I'd be at the fourteenth level."

"What?"

"Later," Fiona said, carelessly waving her hand. "Ronan, will you please get up here?" she yelled, sounding more like a nagging wife than a mystical being.

Sarah Grace looked over the ledge but pulled back as the odor got stronger. A little character no taller than Fiona pulled himself up, huffing and puffing, and clearly unhappy.

"You could have helped me, you know," Ronan complained.

"Sorry," Fiona said sarcastically, "but I broke my wand along the way." Sarah Grace's mind was racing now.

"Wait here, Fiona, I'll be right back."

"Where are you going?"

"I have to go downstairs for a minute, I'll be right back."

Sarah Grace put on her slippers and tiptoed down the stairs to the den to get on the computer. She hoped she wouldn't wake Brucie or Rex who were sleeping in front of the television. As Sarah Grace sat waiting for the computer to power on, she heard noises coming from the kitchen. She suddenly remembered she was supposed to have done the dishes and fed Rex before going to bed. The sounds continued, like someone was sweeping. Sarah Grace turned the computer off quickly, hurried back to her room, and shut the door behind her.

"There's someone in the kitchen," Sarah Grace told Fiona. "It might be a robber or something. And whoever it is, they need a bath."

Fiona snapped her fingers and disappeared. A second later she was back.

"It's Ronan. He's cleaning the kitchen floors."

"But he was just in my bedroom. I didn't see him go past me. My mom's going to freak out when she gets a whiff of that thing."

"Like I said, he's a Grogoch. He's like a leprechaun, but not quite. He's not as clean as they are. He seems pretty nice, but like you already know, he could use a bath."

"Whew!" Sarah Grace said, turning up her nose and stifling a yawn. "How did he do that?"

"Well, SG; it was magic. It's nothing like driving all day in that contraption you were in. Besides, you don't have time for menial chores. You have more important things to do. Oh, and I wouldn't bother trying to look us up on the internet either," Fiona said with a sly smile.

"How did you know what I was doing?" she asked, taking a seat.

Fiona leaned forward and put her elbows on her knees. "It's kind of complicated, and I'll never be able to explain it all at one time, but something is happening to the world around us, and I've got to get you ready."

"Ready for what?"

"To solve the problem."

Sarah Grace was getting a little frustrated and wished this fairy would start stringing some words together. "Fiona, could you please get to the point?"

Fiona sighed deeply. "Sarah Grace, I've got a lot of things to teach you, and if you don't learn them correctly and put them to good use, the world as we know it may not exist in a few months."

"Sarah Grace?" her father called from his bedroom. "Who are you talking to in there?"

She jumped from her seat. "No one Daddy; just reading out loud." When she looked back at her desk, Fiona was gone.

"Ronan, what are you doing, making all this noise down here? You're going to wake up the whole house, and how is SG going to explain this to her parents?"

"Oh, bloody, oh! Just leave me alone, lady. I'm looking for something. Is the little girl asleep?"

"I don't know. Her father called her, so I left. She has a big day ahead of her and she doesn't need you keeping her from getting a good night's sleep."

"Did you tell her?"

"Not exactly."

Ronan's mouth fell open and he regarded Fiona with disbelief. "What do you mean, you didn't tell her? We don't have a lot of time."

"I know that Ronan, but the father interrupted me. I'll just have to explain it tomorrow morning."

"He can't see you anyway," Ronan grumbled, helping himself to the cookie jar. "I've got a big day ahead of me. Maybe I'll find what I'm looking for."

"Ronan, you say that just about every day. What do you mean, 'looking for'?" Fiona asked, more interested in him now. "You didn't even know where you were going. I swear. You have the worst sense of direction."

"I am dreary, I am!" Ronan said, getting irritated.

"Well, look around you, does this place look magical? No! So what could you possibly be looking for?"

Without answering her, Ronan disappeared and found himself in a sea of dolls and stuffed things as he stood in the middle of Sarah Grace's bedroom. Luckily, the girl was asleep.

"Bleck! Cailins!! Why do little girls need such junk?! I bet these animals don't even talk," Ronan mused as he kicked them out of the way and looked for a place to resume his search. Curious now, Fiona hovered just above him. She was determined to find out what he was looking for as she watched him look in every drawer, and at every little thing that had a lid or cover. He had not mentioned anything about something he needed, on the entry into the Littleton's world. She looked at Sarah Grace sleeping soundly in her bed and wondered what she was thinking, and wondered how long she would be laying there with her eyes closed. Fiona sprinkled some twilight dust over the bed only to find herself sliding down the wall opposite the bed after Sarah Grace obliged her with another sneeze.

Sarah Grace awoke feeling strangely well-rested, but she was beginning to wonder if there was insanity in her family. She was sure she'd spoken to a fairy named Fiona and her smelly friend Ronan last night. And what had she been talking about? How was she going to save her world? Sarah Grace put her feet to the floor and stretched her arms above her head. Her arms stayed there for a bit, when she recognized the fairy of her dreams lounging on the floor atop a stuffed animal. Her smelly friend was not far away.

"We thought you'd never wake up," Fiona yawned. "I guess I overdid it with the dust."

"Would you just get on with it?" Ronan demanded. "Her parents will be here any time."

Fiona rubbed her little face, and then floated over to the window. "See that tree?"

Sarah Grace followed her to the window and looked at the huge oak tree across the road. "Sure."

"That's where we live, Ronan and I. It's our entire world, Sarah Grace."

Fiona was beginning to sound a little ominous, Sarah Grace thought nervously.

The little fairy held out her hands and looked around the bedroom. "This is your world. The two of us have to work together to save both."

"Save both? Why? What's going to happen?"

"Someone evil wants to control both," the fairy explained.

"But why?" she asked, stepping back. "I'm no one special. I don't have any magical power."

"Don't you?" Ronan asked, leaning against the wall. "Do you think everyone sees fairies?"

"Well, I....," Sarah Grace began, and then she fell silent. She'd always felt different, but she'd never known why. "Why me?" she asked again.

"I don't know," Fiona said honestly. "Some children are just born with the gift. It's my job to make sure you understand how it works. But before me, it was someone else's job to protect you, a guardian. Your guardian has betrayed us both."

"Do you mean someone wants to hurt me?" she asked, a closed hand to her chest.

"It's possible," said Ronan.

"I don't think I want to know any more," Sarah Grace said, shaking her head.

Fiona felt like doing the same. She was going to have to get past the fear she'd just taught her cailin, if she was ever to gain her trust. "Come with me, Sarah Grace," she said.

"Fiona, you can't!" Ronan insisted.

"It's the only way to make her believe. She believes in us, but not in what we have to do."

"What are you talking about?" the girl asked. "I can't go anywhere. If I miss school…."

"They'll never even know you're gone," Fiona assured her. She disappeared, but returned a moment later.

"Where did you go?" Sarah Grace asked.

"You're family is sleeping in. Come on."

Sarah Grace didn't know how they'd done it, but in the blink of an eye her bedroom disappeared and they were at the base of the old oak tree across the road from the house. She looked down to see Ronan mumbling and arguing with expressive hands and an angry face. Fiona had her arms crossed, having none of it.

"This is a bad idea," Ronan complained. "You know the Queen will not be pleased."

"We're not going to show her everything, just the entrance. We won't even get near the upper chambers. Queen Nivia won't know a thing."

"I love how you like to lie to yourself," Ronan sneered. "It's just a matter of time before we get caught."

"Excuse me," Sarah Grace interrupted, feeling forgotten.

"Ronan, will you just get us in?"

"Fine!" Ronan took what looked like a charcoal pencil from a pouch at his hip. He then drew a series of six symbols at the base of the tree, circles containing stars, triangles, and squares in different combinations. Seconds later, bright light and dust appeared from a small opening in the tree.

Instinctively, Sarah Grace stepped back. Her heart was beating fast, she couldn't even blink her eyes, and she felt her sense of adventure leaving her. She looked back toward her home and wondered if she was ready for the new world she was being offered. Then, she remembered what Fiona had told her the night before. Her guardian had betrayed her. The two of them would have to work together to save both worlds.

"Sarah Grace," Fiona called softly.

Sarah Grace looked down at the little door. "I can't possibly get through there," she said, taking a step back.

"You don't have to go through," Fiona told her. "Just bend down and look."

"And hurry it up," Ronan snapped. I can't keep this door open forever."

Sarah Grace knelt gently before the little door and bent down. Touching her hands to the ground, she put her left eye to the opening and gasped. Through mist she could see a small army of even smaller Grogochs. Some were armed with spears while other seemed to be fortifying a stone wall around the inside perimeter of the tree. They paid no attention to her, but quietly and diligently continued with their work.

"That's enough," said Ronan, and just like that, the door closed.

Sarah Grace sat up and looked at the two.

"Sarah Grace?" Fiona asked with an arched eyebrow.

The girl didn't answer. She just got up and ran across the road to the safety of her home.

But Fiona was wrong. Nivia did know. It wasn't the first time the young fairy had broken a rule, and Nivia knew, smiling to herself, it would not be the last. She admired the rebellious streak which seemed to guide almost everything Fiona did, and Nivia was willing to let it go. After all, she already had an ally in the Littleton home.

Sarah Grace didn't know how she was going to make it through the day. Before she went to bed last night, she'd been the average disgruntled pre-teen, annoyed with school and sometimes with her parents. Now, she was the possessor of some as yet unleashed power, and so many were depending on her. The only thing that could make her feel better now was Wendy.

Wendy was Sarah Grace's best friend and, most of the time, the pair was inseparable. Sarah Grace spent as much time hanging out with Wendy as her parents would allow. Wendy was a foster child, and in the few short years that Sarah Grace knew her, she had been in at least three foster homes. Sarah Grace knew talking about her family made Wendy sad, so she tried not to tell her overly-irritating family stories about her mother and brothers.

Sarah Grace loved Wendy because she seemed to be able to see into the future, and was rarely wrong about the things she claimed to see. Even though both girls were among the popular kids at school, only Sarah Grace was let in on the secrets that Wendy kept. Sarah Grace thought Wendy was the prettiest girl in school, though she would admit she was a little biased. Wendy was shy and sometimes got lost in the class behind all the kids who were much taller than her; but she never seemed to care. Sometimes, Sarah Grace thought she preferred to be invisible. Often Sarah Grace would find Wendy sitting under a tree in the schoolyard, drawing pictures. Wendy was the best student in the art class. She had made many nice clay pots and jewelry.

Sarah Grace spotted her now at the bus stop and ran to greet her. She couldn't get there fast enough to tell her about her crazy night. Sarah Grace stopped short as she approached her friend, and saw the sad look in her eyes.

"What's the matter, Wendy?" Sarah Grace asked.

"My foster parents are going to send me away at the end of the school year."

"How do you know that? Did they say something to you?"

"No; I just know they are. I've been having dreams again. It happens every time I have to move. I'm not sure, but I think Father Francis has something to do with it."

"Father Francis? What would he want with you? He's not supposed to have children."

"No, I think he's going to try to get me taken away."

"Until your foster parents tell you differently, I don't think you should pay too much attention to that particular dream." Sarah Grace knew for a fact that Wendy's foster parents wanted very much to adopt her. They'd been foster parents for years to many children, but at this stage in their lives, Wendy was their only charge, and they'd developed a special relationship with her. The only thing keeping them from legally adopting Wendy was the Welfare Department. The social worker who placed Wendy with them was concerned they might be too old to raise a little girl.

"Besides, Father Francis doesn't even like kids. I don't know why he's even at the church. He needs to go back to the priest-making place and do whatever they do there. I think your dreams are getting cloudy. You might hate your life, but you don't want mine," Sarah Grace assured her. "You'd have to put up with two smelly brothers. I wish I could change my family once in awhile."

"I guess you're right. I'll worry about that tomorrow. Did you see the new boy? He's not as cute as Marissa said he was. His eyes don't fit his head right."

Sarah Grace laughed. Her friend may be shy, but never afraid to speak her mind when they were in private. "Devon's some kind of alien. I wish he'd jump back on his spaceship and head back to his home planet." Both girls laughed and raced inside to beat the morning bell.

"I'm sorry to have to bother you with this, Mother Superior," Lt. Christopher said, taking a seat opposite the desk. "My officers have removed the body and we've taken every step not to disrupt the children's school day."

Mother Superior stood by the window and watched Sarah Grace and Wendy walking into the school. Warm feelings she'd once had for Sarah Grace Littleton were becoming twisted, and resentment was setting in. Sarah Grace would know exaltation. It was likely she never would, Mother Superior thought bitterly.

Taking out his notebook, Lt. Christopher jotted down some notes. "Now, Mother Superior, you're sure you don't recognize our John Doe from the photographs I showed you?"

She turned to her desk and sat down. "As I told you, I've never seen him before. But of course, there is a church here. Many strangers come and go without notice. We're much more careful at the school, however, and there is a security guard and a night watchman to protect the children and the property. Haven't you been able to identify this poor man through fingerprints, or perhaps dental records?"

The detective's face was troubled as he looked up from his notes. "He has neither."

"Mother Superior?" It was Sister Mary Beth. "Is everything okay?"

"Yes, Sister; what is it?"

"Bishop Mark Andrew asked to speak with you immediately."

"What does he need? I am very busy this morning."

"I did not ask, Mother Superior, and he did not offer an explanation."

"Very well, Sister, you may be excused."

"Thank you Mother Superior. Oh, and if I may say so," Sister Mary Beth added, looking over Mother Superior's shoulder, "that Wendy sure is a blessing isn't she? It's a shame they can't find a good home for her."

"Yes, yes it is," Mother Superior responded slowly, as she turned back to look over the schoolyard. Wendy and Sarah Grace had attended the Holy Heart of Mary School together for five years.

Mother Superior hurried now to Bishop Mark Andrew's office, hoping her delay would not upset him terribly. The Bishop was not known for his patience with the nuns. Oh, he was very kind, but if he said to come at 10:00, he did not mean 10:01, or sometime around 10:00; he meant what he said.

"Mother Superior, you are late," Bishop Mark Andrew said without looking up.

"My apologies, Bishop. It won't happen again."

"Of course. To the business at hand, we'll need to do

everything we can to reassure the parents and the public about this unfortunate business. You've met with the detective. Is there anything new to report?"

"Not at present, your Excellency. I do believe any problems will be short in duration. A man has died, God rest his soul, but this is a rather large area. He could have come from anywhere and crossed paths with almost anyone. Our most difficult task will be keeping the children focused, and dispelling any rumors among them."

"An astute observation, Reverend Mother. I'll leave it in your capable hands. I'm sure the authorities will contact us if there is anything further. Now, tell me, who is responsible for the holy water in the Narthex?"

And just like that, the conversation returned to the more mundane tasks tackled by the staff on a daily basis. That's where the problem lay. To her shame, she found herself increasingly bored with her life as a nun. Devotion to her young charges had once been challenging, but the challenges had become much like the seasons. A constant round of perpetual ceremony, which left little to her imagination, anymore.

Assuring the Bishop she'd deal with the holy water situation as well, Mother Superior returned to her office, tossing a heavy set of keys onto her desk. A trapping of her office, she got to hold a key to every lock on the campus. How illustrious she was, she thought sarcastically.

Sister Mary Beth entered the room unannounced, as she did usually. "The mail, Mother Superior," she said, leaving a large bundle of envelopes on the desk. The little nun disappeared as quickly as she had appeared, as was also her custom.

She sat down and went through the pile of correspondence. New catalogs for books, kitchen supplies, and school spirit items, were the usual fare. Her hand stopped in mid-air as she observed one envelope in particular. It was expensive stationery; heavy, with a raised design, addressed to her; obviously by a calligrapher, and with no return address. She didn't normally receive mail of a personal nature, as she had no real family to speak of.

Mother Superior opened the envelope carefully, as if it were a delicate gift of crystal wrapped in rose petals. It read simply:

"I offer what you seek.

I will see you tonight, 7PM, at the bell tower.

Bring only your courage."

Her first instinct was to throw the letter away. It was obviously meant for someone else. But as her hand was ferrying it to the wastepaper basket, she stopped and slowly brought the letter back to the desk. Mother Superior looked at that pile of dirty keys and the stack of letters. Something in her recoiled. She read the letter again, and then stuffed it into a pocket in her habit. Was it a date with destiny? She felt she was ready to find out.

Even with his limited ability to change size, Branduff watched the woman from a distant corner of the room, clinging playfully from a piece of wooden architecture he found rough hewn and lacking artistically. This woman was hungry, and desperate for things outside her usual world. She would be willing to do almost anything to achieve it. This time, he knew he'd chosen well.

Chapter 3

In class later that day, Sarah Grace and Wendy sat side by side during grammar class. Sarah Grace had felt the need to look over her shoulder most of the day. Fiona had not made an appearance, and Sarah Grace still couldn't be one hundred percent sure that this morning's happenings had in fact been genuine.

Before the spelling test, Wendy said a prayer of peace, so she wouldn't be nervous. Sarah Grace didn't quite understand the effectiveness of prayer, so she reached into her sweater pocket and clutched her pet rock, hoping she would have enough luck to get a perfect score on the test.

Sarah Grace's brothers had tried unsuccessfully to take the rock from her over the years, but they weren't as quick as her, which made them try all the more. Sarah Grace knew that luck was just a way to trick her mind into believing in the impossible, but it provided enough security for her to get her through many uncertain situations. There was nothing special about her rock, and she thought the same of some of Wendy's prayers. Both girls acted according to what they believed, and took the test.

Sarah Grace couldn't help thinking about what Wendy had

told her when she got off the bus that morning. She tried to imagine what life must be like for her having to move all the time, and have different moms and dads. Sarah Grace loved her family and often wished she could be rid of her brothers, but as she thought about this now, she hoped she would never have to know what being without her family was like. But now, she also felt even more protective of Wendy and her family. Looking through the hall of the school, watching the children go by, she felt more protective of them as well.

The school was finally quiet. At 6:50 P.M., Mother Superior reached into her pocket and patted the letter, wondering if it was in fact real, wondering if she truly had the courage to meet this stranger. What was she thinking? What if this person had something to do with the man who'd been killed? She could be taking her life into her own hands -- at the promise of what?

In a distinct moment of clarity, she shook off any remaining doubts and headed toward the bell tower. She stopped at the fountain in the Rosary Garden just long enough to keep the other nuns from being suspicious. The wind had picked up, so she made her way with her head down. As she hurried, her heart raced in anticipation of what was about to happen.

"Oh! Ouch!" Mother Superior felt herself falling quickly to the ground. When she looked up, there was no one there. She looked around again to see what she might have run into, and wasn't sure if she had hit it, or if it had run into her. Whatever it was, or whoever it was, was gone now. Certainly she could not have tripped on anything; there were no trees or benches around. She picked herself up and continued to the steps of the bell tower.

Fiona floated to the edge of the garden, laughing hysterically.

Ronan watched her little amusement. "It's gonna take more than tripping a nun to solve this problem."

"Oh, Ronan," Fiona giggled, "you've gotta lighten up."

"I'll lighten up when you get to work, Fiona. All you've done is make contact with Sarah Grace and scare the girl to death. She doesn't have any idea of what she needs to do or how to do it. I wouldn't care so much except that until you're done, I can't go back to my own life."

"You don't have to stay with me," Fiona threw at him.

"Ha!! I guess that's one of those little things you missed over the last two thousand years. When Queen Nivia said you could take me with you, she meant I had to go with you and help. She meant," he said, the volume of his voice increasing along with the agitation, "that I was supposed to stay with you until the job was accomplished, and that if it wasn't, I would be in just as much trouble as you."

Fiona straightened up and let the tips of her wings skim her hands.

She regarded Ronan with some concern. He was a pretty serious Grogoch and she didn't want to tease him. But if she was going to make this work, she would have to do it her way.

Mother Superior managed the last few steps to the bell tower, stunned her knees could complete the climb, but pure adrenaline kept her going. In her younger days, she had passed many an afternoon here with the other sisters, and thought it the most tranquil spot on the entire facility. From the bell tower, you could see a good deal of the county and its numerous farms, spread out like the squares on a patchwork quilt. For a minute, she felt the calm of her younger days; but it was soon replaced by a sense of dread. What was she doing here? Was the need to distinguish herself, so great that she was willing to risk the modest gains of her life?

The wind picked up and the dead fall leaves began to swirl

around her in a torrent of color. The diminutive tornado took on a life of its own, swirling higher and higher, until she felt the need to cover her eyes and mouth, before the dust threatened to choke her. She was being warned, she thought to herself. The force behind the leaves was only gaining strength, and in her attempt to back away from it, she tripped on the hem of her habit and went tumbling to the ground.

Winded and bruised, she immediately resolved to forget about the letter, as well as the elusive offer she'd been made.

"Don't be too hasty, Mother Superior."

The wind died down and the leaves finally found rest on the stone floor around them. Mother Superior lowered her hands; blinking, because she could still feel bits of dust in her eyes.

"Let me help you," the voice said.

His voice was like polished silk; smooth and rich.

Her eyes opened slowly, and she saw a hand coming toward her face.

"Please. Take my hand," he said. "Don't be afraid."

Mother Superior looked up. It was an early moon which framed the back of the man's head, and his facial features were barely visible. She took the hand offered. It was manicured and soft. She thought he had to be a professional man. He carefully lifted her to her feet, and helped her find support on one of the wooden posts used to hold up the turreted roof of the bell tower.

"Are you injured?"

Looking herself over momentarily, she quickly shook her head. She realized he had not released her hand. As she started to pull it away, his grip tightened.

"Why should you want to pull away? I believe I'm the lifeline you've been asking for." With a reassuring smile, he gently released her hand and stepped back.

With each step he took, more and more, the features of his face were detailed. And with each step, the ability to speak failed her. The face wasn't like anything she'd ever seen before. Skin she'd expected to be brown or pink, was almost translucent. There was a nose, two ears and two eyes, but the eyes had no pupils, no life, and no glint of humanity. She tried to back away, but the rigid wooden post behind her made that impossible. Mother Superior was already regretting her hasty decision to change her own fate.

Branduff had already detected her fear. "You needn't worry.

I'm quite harmless."

"Who -- what -- are you?" she asked defensively.

"Remember, Mother Superior, it was *you* whose wishes summoned *me*."

"That isn't true," she insisted. "You sent the letter to me."

"And how would I have known that you're unhappy with your lot in life?"

"I don't know! I have no idea. I've never spoken to you a day in my life."

"You didn't need to speak. I was able to read your thoughts."

Mother Superior tore herself away from that post with sheer will, and made her way hastily to the staircase, but jumped back when a wood beam fell to block her way. She looked back to see the thing lowering his arm.

"It is not my desire that you should leave before we have talked, Mother Superior."

She stepped back again, to a corner as far away from him as she could get. "You want something. What is it? Who are you?"

"Who I am is unimportant. What I can offer you is."

"You killed that man, didn't you?" she asked, the inevitable sense of stupidity rushing over her for being here. "You're the one the police are looking for."

"They'll be chasing their tails long after our business is completed."

"What business? Would you please stop talking in riddles? Tell me what you want, so I can leave!!"

He took measured steps toward her, a smile playing upon his lips. "We have so much to offer one another," he said. "I have need of immortality. You have need of acknowledgment, and a place in the light."

She stiffened. "It's clear you're not human. Why would you need my assistance to become immortal?"

Branduff laughed. "You endow me with more power than even I can imagine. Alas, there are some things I cannot achieve on my own. In order to gain immortality, I'll need the innocent essence of a mortal child. And as you might have guessed, in my world, those are few."

Every conceivable depravity suddenly raced through her mind, and she was even more ashamed she'd let herself be drawn into this. Not only had she failed herself, she'd exposed the children and the school to someone – something -- which was an abomination.

"Calm yourself, Mother Superior. I'm little affected by the weaknesses of mortal men. What we both wish to attain is far beyond that, isn't it?" he asked, moving within inches of her face.

His eyes were now glowing red and she could not tear her eyes away. She was trapped, physically and mentally, within his gaze and the tight perimeter of the bell tower. Mother Superior gasped as its hand neared her face. And then, it spoke:

"Strong of mind, yet faint of heart,

On this night, your worlds will part,

Take my hand and surrender now,

To mine own will, shall be your vow."

Words from a creature which may have once repulsed her, were now received with joy. Fear dissolved into excitement; excitement over the idea of achieving something more than this mundane existence. Her expression relaxed in his gaze. "Yes, Your Excellency."

"I'm so pleased, Mother Superior. Yes, I think we shall work well together." He took her hand and drew her to the center of the turret. He'd so easily placed himself in the scheme of her world, and she now regarded him as a higher authority figure than the Bishop. But then again, that was the frustrating thing about his power. He could change shape. He could twist a simpler mind to his will. Unfortunately, it was forbidden, even for him, to interfere directly in the lives of humans. Oh, no. That was reserved for Nivia. That's why he desperately needed this woman's assistance. He needed a child. She would get it for him.

Father Francis was new to the school, hired as the disciplinarian and substitute history teacher. So far, he'd received mix reviews from the parishioners. While the children seemed to like him, some parents and older churchgoers were taking a "wait and see" attitude. But, Father Francis was aware of the innuendo and was determined to not let any of that prevent him from his purpose for being there. He watched with curiosity for a moment, as Mother Superior hurried through the garden.

Returning to her room, Mother Superior was surprised to see a pouch sitting on the edge of her dresser. Confused, she picked it up and looked inside. Even in the dimly lit room, she could see something twinkling in the bottom of the dark bag. Turning it upside down, a diamond the size of a small egg filled her palm.

She caught her breath. Rolling the precious gem in her hand, feeling its weight, she knew it had to be worth thousands, perhaps tens of thousands of dollars.

There was something else in the bag. A small card with a note scribbled across it. Switching on the lamp on her desk, she read: *"Something to show my appreciation."* It was from him.

Fiona sat at the top of the mirror in Mother Superior's room, very curious about what the nun had up her sleeve and where she'd gotten that pouch. It was a Fae gem pouch. She had seen Mother Superior glaring at Wendy and Sarah Grace that morning. She arrived just in time to hear Sister Elizabeth talk about Wendy. Fiona did not see anything particularly special about Wendy. She was quiet and reserved, but after hearing her name mentioned, there must be something more to Wendy than anyone could see. Fiona did her best to keep out of private matters, but she had not had much exposure to humans, and there was something about Mother Superior she did not like. She was curious; so much so that she looked over Mother Superior's shoulder, as she read that note. The note made little sense, but the woman reacted as though she had been handed the key to a thousand secrets. She smiled to herself as she thought about how she had caused the nun to fall in the Rosary Garden.

The wind was only supposed to last an hour, but Fiona had accidentally ordered it to blow until sunrise, and considering her last misguided trip on the wind, she thought it best to take cover.

Fiona had been reading some of the books in Mother Superior's room while waiting for her to return and learned that nuns are not allowed any luxuries. In the last few hours, she had come to like hanging out with Sarah Grace and was becoming very protective of her.

Sarah Grace's mother had allowed her to spend the night with Wendy and attend midnight mass. Normally, she was not allowed to be up that late, but since she was at a friend's house, she was permitted to do what the family did. Sarah Grace's family always went to Mass on Wednesday nights and Sunday mornings. As soon as Sarah Grace set foot in Wendy's bedroom, she felt a tug on her shirt collar.

"Psst!" Fiona hissed.

"What? Fiona, you're going to be seen," Sarah Grace warned.

"Only if you want me to be seen," she said.

"What?"

"It's one of your powers," Fiona explained. "To give fairy

sight to anyone you feel needs it. It might be a good idea to let Wendy see."

"What about Ronan? Where is he?"

"Oh, he won't be coming. Grogochs don't like priests. And, since he knows we're going to Mass, he'll keep his distance."

"How come he doesn't like priests? Did he used to be one? He probably got kicked out of the church for smelling so bad, huh?" Fiona and Sarah Grace giggled.

"What are you laughing about and who were you talking to? " Wendy asked.

Sarah Grace thought about it for a moment. "Okay, Fiona, let her see you. " In a gentle explosion of golden dust, Fiona made herself visible to Wendy. "Ummm, Fiona, this is my friend, Wendy. Wendy, this is Fiona. She's a real fairy!"

"Oh my gosh! A real live fairy? Can I touch you?" Wendy asked, excitedly.

"No, you can't touch me," Fiona said, offended, and flew back to Sarah Grace. "SG, tell your friend that I am not a toy," she whispered.

"Aww, c'mon Fiona. You let me touch you."

"Yes, but that is only when I needed help after your fatal sneezes in the middle of the night."

"Where did she come from? Why are you here?" Wendy asked, the questions coming faster than she could think them up.

"It's complicated," said Sarah Grace.

"You can say that again," Fiona agreed. "But since you're SG's best friend, you'll probably have to see me on occasion."

"Sarah Grace, you're so lucky," Wendy bemoaned. "You have everything." She reached out a tentative finger to convince herself the little fairy truly existed.

Sarah Grace watched her with a mixture of confusion and sadness. Was she really lucky? She truly wondered about that all the while Fiona had been explaining what she was. She'd never heard of a person who could see fairies, but apparently they were all around her. While that was mystical and wonderful, the excitement had turned to worry when Fiona told her about the others, the enemies. The idea of coming face to face with a Droch, or even a changeling frightened her. She wanted the magic, but did she want the responsibility that went along with it?

Then she looked over at Wendy, gently touching Fiona's

wings; and in that moment, she did feel blessed. Her family got on her nerves, without a doubt, but she'd be lost without them. Why had she been graced with this special power and what could she do with it?

Fiona rolled her eyes, and stood up on the edge of the dresser. "You two need to listen. There could be trouble and it includes both of you."

The girls looked at each other and sat on the bed, barely able to contain themselves. Sarah Grace was excited to be a part of a problem she didn't completely understand, and Wendy was terrified that she was part of a problem she didn't even know about. Both of them had questions piling up in their brains, as they hoped Fiona would talk faster.

"Well, there was a note, and Mother Superior, and Bishop Mark Andrew…" Fiona wasn't known for her great ability to tell stories.

"Bishop? Are you sure it wasn't Father Francis?" Wendy challenged.

"Yes, I'm sure, now let me finish, please."

Wendy slouched, wondering how her vision could have been wrong. She was never wrong.

"Ahem." Fiona continued. "There were those people and something about some papers from the social worker with Wendy's name on them." Fiona studied the stunned looks on the faces of the girls, as they hung on every word.

Had Wendy's vision been correct? Sarah Grace wondered to herself. But if it were true, what did Bishop Mark Andrew have to do with anything? None of this made sense to her, but she would find a way to get answers before the end of the school year. She was not about to lose her friend, and certainly not to a woman with the likes of Mother Superior. No one liked her, but this was one more reason to find out what the old nun was up to. She would start at midnight Mass.

Back on the farm, Ronan was having a heyday. Glad to be rid of Sarah Grace and Fiona for a while, he busied himself with finding what he had come for. It turns out that he had not been misguided by the wind, he had only gotten his messages confused; something that happened often; but he stopped to thank whatever was looking out for him and steered him in the right direction.

Ronan thought it quite funny that he happened upon two girls who went to church all the time. He didn't care a whip about church and couldn't stand the priests, but he knew enough about it to know that some humans claimed to have been healed by the priests that visited them. It made perfect sense that he would find the power of healing somewhere near the priests.

As he tore through Sarah Grace's belongings again, he was more determined than ever to find a clue as to where he could find what he was looking for. He wasn't exactly sure what he was looking for, but he was sure he would know it when he got to it. The stories he heard about its great power were enough to keep him digging for clues. He left nothing unturned, and by the time he was finished, there were socks on the lampshades, and shirts and hangers in the trash. There wasn't a bare spot on the floor, but he didn't notice until Mrs. Littleton came in and saw the mess he had made. She muttered her disgust at the sight and the odor in the room, and left as quickly as she had come.

Ronan looked around, a little embarrassed at what he had done. He couldn't have this girl in trouble. She was going to have enough challenges. With three blinks and a whistle, each item returned to its place, and the room was clean again. Ronan smiled to himself and lay down in the closet to take a nap.

Wendy sat on the edge of her bed and by habit, grabbed the

necklace she had worn for as long as she could remember. The necklace was the only thing that traveled with her from foster home to foster home. Someone told her that her parents had left it with her when they left her at the church, when she was a baby. Wendy knew that there was something special about the locket she wore around her neck. She was never able to open it but found the two rubies on the cover more beautiful than anything else. As she touched the stones, she imagined that she was with her family somewhere, about to go to Mass.

"See what you did, Fiona? You made her sad," Sarah Grace said, grabbing her friend's hand. "Why do we have to think about this right now? We're supposed to be getting ready to go."

"Because," said Fiona, "Wendy could be gone if we don't do something. Now, I happen to know that Mother Superior met with someone tonight. I think that same someone gave her a gift."

"What do you mean, 'someone'?" Wendy asked.

"Well, I can't be everywhere. Someone has to keep an eye on Ronan, who hasn't appeared yet... I wonder what he's up to."

Wendy threw Sarah Grace another look of surprise, feeling more left out of this little plan than before. "Who is Ronan?"

Sarah Grace shrugged. "You'll know when he's here. He's almost impossible to ignore."

Wendy wrinkled her nose and checked the clock. "Okay, let's go. We don't want to be late like Sarah Grace is all the time." Wendy looked over her shoulder at Fiona and whispered to Sarah Grace, "What are we going to do with her while we're gone?"

"Don't worry. No one but us can see or hear her. Just be careful to not talk to her when other people are around. They might think we're crazy or something."

The girls finished getting ready as Fiona watched, wondering how it was that they could exist without magic and dust. Their lives would be so much easier if they did things the easy way, she thought, as she followed the girls to the church. As they entered the sanctuary, both girls immediately gazed up at Mother Superior in the choir loft. The aging nun sat without expression, looking at the girls briefly, and then turning her head to whisper something to one of the other sisters.

A child, Mother Superior thought to herself. My new master needs a child. One who is pure of heart, one who is not troublesome, one who will obey. That description certainly did not fit Sarah Grace; but, Wendy, on the other hand.....

From the other side of the church, Father Francis sat watching Mother Superior with great intrigue. She seemed to be eyeing the two girls walking down the aisle. Father Francis watched as Mother Superior watched, never taking her eyes off of the girls until the service was almost over. Even as he sang the liturgy, he noticed she took an exceptional interest in these two children.

He tried to focus on the service, but couldn't help but notice that Mother Superior was gone after the offering was collected. He stood, wishing he could follow her, unaware that one of the two girls was thinking the very same thing.

Sarah Grace excused herself to the restroom and walked out the side door to the hallway. She was not sure which way to go, so she headed to the front of the church until she heard voices in one of the hallways leading to the offices. Sarah Grace walked quickly, as she would be missed soon. But she did not have to wait long, before she walked upon a hushed conversation. It was rude to listen, but once she recognized the back of Mother Superior, she couldn't help herself.

Her back to the wall, she inched slowly toward the woman who was speaking to some man. The man's face was not visible, and all Sarah Grace could really make out was that he wore a dark suit and had a very deep and almost mesmerizing voice. But she wasn't close enough, and the words they spoke were too muffled. The only thing she could make out were the words, 'girl' and 'adoption'".

Sarah Grace turned to run as she heard footsteps. She slid into a hall closet just in time to see Mother Superior running down the hall to her office. Sarah Grace wanted to follow her, but knew she needed to get back to the service before it ended and she was left to explain herself once again.

As she turned to leave, she ran right into Devon. "What do you want?" she complained, already annoyed at the idea of this conversation.

"Oh, to know what you're up to," he asked, walking behind her and glancing down the hall. "You've already been missed in the chapel."

"Great," she moaned.

"Sarah Grace, I get the feeling you don't like me too much," he smirked, sarcasm written all over that remark.

"You only get a feeling?" she teased, rolling her eyes. If she had to be honest, Devon wasn't a bad looking boy, but she just wasn't interested in boys right now. That was even before she let a fairy into her life.

Both children jumped as they heard a noise, and were reminded they weren't where they were supposed to be. They ran back to the chapel just before the service ended.

Chapter 4

Mother Superior sat at her desk and pulled a file from one of the lower drawers. Someone knocked on her door, which startled her and made her shriek, dropping the file on the floor.

Father Francis opened the door quickly. "Mother Superior, are you all right?" he asked, rushing in.

"Father Francis!" Mother Superior exclaimed. "I'm sorry, you surprised me. Yes, yes, all is well," she assured him, leaving her chair to retrieve the papers she'd dropped.

"Oh, let me help you," he offered, reaching for the papers strewn all over the floor.

"Oh no, that's not necessary."

But he already had the papers in his hands. "Adoption? Have you found a home for one of our foster children?" he asked, hopeful.

"Possibly," she lied, averting her gaze to the top of the desk. Whether she was under Branduff's control or not, she found it hard to lie to a priest. "I was hoping to find a home for Wendy."

"Wendy, Wendy," he wondered aloud. "Sarah Grace

Littleton's best friend?"

She shook her head. "Yes. She desperately wants a home of her own. I thought I'd make a more concentrated search."

"Good luck. Finding adoptive families for older children is always hard. I suppose her foster family is not interested in a permanent situation?"

"Ah…no, of course," Mother Superior stammered. Another lie.

"Well, I wish you luck, Mother Superior. Please let me know if there's anything I can do to help. Have a good evening."

"Good night, Father." Mother Superior dropped into her chair as soon as the door thudded shut.

Mother Superior slept fitfully that night, tossing and turning in her sleep. She dreamt of the craziest creatures, things the children would read about in a fairy tale. The creatures were chasing her, pointing at her, and calling her names she didn't understand. She awoke several times to find her sheets crumpled on the floor, and an eerie feeling that she was not alone in her room. Sometimes, the sheets seemed to be floating over the bed away from her. When she turned on the light, there was no one there;, only the discomforting silence she had once appreciated.

Days on the tree farm began early. Mr. Littleton had a small staff of three men who helped with the heavy work, as well as an arborist, who was like a tree doctor, to make sure the stock remained healthy. Her brothers did a few chores, like watering and loading the trucks, before they set off for school, but Sarah Grace usually helped her Grammy with the small shrubs and ornamental flowers.

Sarah Grace was quiet this morning and her grandmother had noticed. "What's wrong, Bumblebee?" she asked, pushing the old straw hat back on her head. "Worried about your boyfriend?" she chuckled.

Sarah Grace gave her grandmother a tiresome look and finished stacking her plants along the wall of the greenhouse. She was bothered by quite a few things, none of which she felt she could share. Grammy would think she was crazy. Of course, her Grammy was the craziest person in the house, so she might just understand. But Sarah Grace took a moment to reconsider confiding in her aging soul mate, when she noticed her kissing the butterfly which had landed on her now delicate and frail hands.

She doted on the little insect as if it were one of her

grandchildren, then flung her hand into the air and sent her new friend on its way. "It's fairy season all right," she nodded with certainty.

"But Grammy, it's gonna get cool soon and the butterflies will be leaving."

"Fairy season's got nothing to do with the weather, child."

Sarah Grace had been hearing her grandmother talk about fairy season ever since she could remember. She just thought she liked to make up stories to entertain the kids. Sarah Grace didn't know what other kids' grandmothers were like, but she knew hers was special.

"Bus, Sarah Grace," her mother said, coming out the side door and handing the girl her book bag and lunch. "I put an extra cookie in there for Wendy."

"Thanks, Momma. She'll like that."

"If ever a child needed extra mothering, it's Wendy," said Grammy. "You two are practically sisters."

"I know," Sarah Grace said proudly. "I wish she did live with us."

"Don't worry," Velvet told her daughter. "A home for Wendy

will come along. You just have to have faith."

The big yellow bus came to a halt in front of the house with a squeal and a groan. Sarah Grace fully believed that one day it would rattle apart. She kissed her mother and grandmother good-bye and ran to board the bus, waving to Wendy, who was practically hanging out of a window. She obviously had some gossip to share.

"Hey SG, it's time to go," Fiona said, flying around the kitchen table as Sarah Grace ate her breakfast. "Hurry up, we've got to go now."

"Shhh!" Sarah Grace hissed.

"What's wrong with you, Sis?" Brucie asked. "Are the little voices in your head getting too loud?"

"Shut up, Brucie," Fiona mumbled.

Fiona walked over to his juice glass and kicked it over. Sarah Grace hid her face in her napkin to keep from laughing at the mess dripping into her brother's lap. She excused herself and went to get her schoolbooks.

On the way to the bus stop, Fiona told Sarah Grace what had happened the night before, and Sarah Grace shared what she had seen after Mass on Saturday night.

"What are we going to do, Fiona?" Sarah Grace asked.

"I don't know, but we have to get to school fast, and that bus isn't going to get us there fast enough. Where is Ronan...?"

At the mention of his name, Ronan appeared in a ball of dust, the same dust ball that Sarah Grace had seen rolling next to her car last week. When the dust settled, Sarah Grace stood in the driveway, shocked at what she saw standing in front of her. There was a little man who stood no taller than her waist. At least she thought he was a little man, it was hard to tell under the thick reddish brown hair all over his body. He wore only a pair of trousers and suspenders. Sarah Grace wished he had chosen to put some shoes on because his feet were also covered with the same thick hair over the long, flat feet.

Sarah Grace stood with her hand over her nose hoping this stinky little man would not attempt to touch her. Ronan reminded her of a cranky uncle who smoked smelly cigars and was constantly shooing his nieces and nephews away.

"We have to get to the school, pronto; and we need you to come with us to help out SG's little friend."

"Where are we going today?" Ronan asked as he fruitlessly

dusted off his jacket.

"To the Holy Heart of Mary Catholic School, please," Sarah Grace said through her hand.

"Oh, no, I'm not going anywhere near that place. There are priests and things. I am not going in there," Ronan said nervously.

"You don't have to go in," said Fiona. "You can stay outside. You'll be of good use to us there, anyway."

"Outside for what? What's happening?"

"I'll explain on the way," Fiona said.

And in the snap of a finger, Sarah Grace was standing in front of her school, leaving Rex standing in the driveway barking, wondering where his friend had gone in such a hurry.

"That was totally awesome!" Sarah Grace squealed. "We have to do that again."

"We don't have time to play SG, we have to find your friend."

"But she's not here yet. She should be on the bus. Since I got here in a blink, we have to wait for her," Sarah Grace explained.

"Great, while the two of you are waiting, I am going to the

other side of the street. Shout when you need me," Ronan said, disappearing again.

They only had a few minutes before class started, but Fiona and the girls were eager to know what Mother Superior was doing. Fiona had put off the distressing news for as long as she could, but Sarah Grace needed to be told. She had a lot to learn, and the Summer Solstice would be upon them before they knew it.

"We're not supposed to be up here," Wendy warned, looking over her shoulder. "If we get caught, we could be on detention for weeks."

"She's right, Fiona," Sarah Grace agreed, shaking her head. "Students aren't supposed to be anywhere near the nuns' cells."

"Cells?" the fairy asked. "Isn't that what they put humans in when they've done something bad?" Fiona considered the idea for a moment. "How ironic," she observed with dry sarcasm.

The girls looked at one another, then back at the fairy floating in front of them. But upon hearing footsteps behind them, the three ducked into a dark alcove and held their breaths.

Mother Superior hastily moved through the hall to her cell and unlocked the heavy oak door. Though, as sparsely furnished as the other nuns' cells, this one was a little larger and was afforded a small desk and telephone. Once in, she closed the door.

"How are we going to see anything now?" Sarah Grace asked.

Fiona pulled a flower bud from her pouch and gently launched it into the air. The bud grew, the petals opened, and a translucent ball floated before them.

"This is too cool," Wendy gasped.

"We can see what she's doing!" Sarah Grace exclaimed. "Can she see us?"

"No," Fiona told them.

For the next couple of minutes they watched Mother Superior move around her cell, remove the large jewel from a desk drawer and put it into a black bag. She tucked the bag under her habit and left the room.

Fiona closed the petals of the flower and tucked it away.

"I don't know a lot about nuns," said Wendy, "but I do know they're not supposed to have fancy stuff."

Sarah Grace had gone strangely quiet as a sickening sense of dread folded in on her.

"What's wrong, Sarah Grace?" Fiona asked, though she already knew the answer.

"She's my guardian, isn't she?"

"Yes," came the solemn reply.

The rest of the day went by in a fog for Sarah Grace. She didn't hear anything anyone else said. She couldn't recall the taste of her food, and only barely responded to questions. With every little detail, she learned about her future, she was more and more desperate to return to the past. Stepping off the school bus that day, she would have given anything to erase the past few days, and once again become the girl who was in trouble at school for not paying attention.

As the bus roared away with its noisy cargo, Sarah Grace went over to the old oak tree and sat down. Fiona was there moments later.

"You always know when to show up and when to disappear, don't you?" Sarah Grace asked.

"I thought you needed some time to yourself. I think I know how you feel."

"How?" Sarah Grace demanded. "You don't have parents,

brothers, or best friends. You don't have to depend on others to take care of you, and look after you. And when someone lets you down, you don't have to feel like, like….."

"Like you've been betrayed?" Fiona demanded, floating away to a more comfortable distance. "You think I don't know disappointment and betrayal? You think that during the two thousand years of my life, I've never had someone turn on me, and shake my confidence and faith? You're not even what humans consider an adult, but you think you can tell me what I already know?"

Sarah Grace's chest was rising and falling rapidly and her eyes were narrowed, trying to hold back the tears.

Fiona tried to fly away, but stopped mid air and turned back to her small charge. "That's why I need your help, Sarah Grace. You're a chosen one. Someone saw something very special in you. You were chosen because that someone knew you could make a difference."

"You mean, like God?" the child wondered aloud.

"In your world, maybe. In our world, the Queen, maybe. She speaks to all. She is powerful, but she is not arrogant. She doesn't pretend to possess all. Maybe it was from her lips to

God's ear," Fiona giggled. And to her delight, Sarah Grace giggled as well.

"Now what?" the cailin asked.

Fiona buzzed downward and landed in the girl's hand. "Tomorrow, the real work begins."

Sarah Grace took a deep cleansing breath, picked up her book bag and headed across the road with Fiona resting gently on her shoulder. "You know, you've got a lot of attitude for a fairy."

"Comes with the wings."

Chapter 5

Brucie and Jonathan watched Sarah Grace with new curiosity. Brothers didn't usually pay much attention to a sister unless some serious teasing was underfoot, but even they were beginning to notice something different about her. Over the last few days, she'd become quieter, and was keeping to herself more. On occasion, Sarah Grace had even seemed sad. Yes; they were paying a little more attention to their sister because of her mood, but mostly they were paying a little more attention this morning, because they'd never seen anyone gobble down pancakes like that.

"Sarah Grace, slow down," her mother scolded. "The food's not going anywhere." Velvet sat down next to her husband and poured herself a cup of coffee.

"Oh, she's just got a healthy appetite," Grammy said. "God knows she could use a little meat on her bones," the older woman laughed.

"Momma, don't forget your doctor's appointment this afternoon," Velvet reminded her mother.

It took Grammy a split second to go from happy to indignant. "I don't need to see the doctor. I was just a little dizzy, that's all.

I just got out of bed too fast."

"For goodness sake, Gram," Melvin teased, "you treat going to the doctor like you're standing in front of a firing squad."

"Once they pull out the needles, there's not much difference," she grimaced.

Sarah Grace laughed as Grammy poked her in the side.

Saturday mornings were usually a relaxing time for kids, but not when they lived on a farm. Education was very important to the Littletons, but the farm was their livelihood, and on the weekends, everyone was expected to pitch in to get the work done. While more was required of the boys outside, Sarah Grace had her own list of chores, inside and out. Therein lay the first problem. How was she going to get out of her chores?

"You boys finish up," said Daddy. "We've got that whole back field to work on today. Summer's coming and there's a lot of weeding and mulching to do."

The groans bounced off every wall of the kitchen. "How long, Dad?" Jonathan asked.

"As long as it takes," Mr. Littleton said matter-of-factly.

Sarah Grace knew she could get away with a lot when it came

to her Dad, but no one got out of the Saturday chores. Trying to think of an excuse, Sarah Grace glanced over to the window and saw Ronan sitting on the window sill, swinging his legs. He tipped his hat and winked.

"Momma, may I…."

"Yes."

Sarah Grace was almost stunned into silence. "But I haven't even asked for anything yet."

"Yes, you can go," her father said.

They didn't even seem to hear her. Sarah Grace looked back at Ronan, who winked at her again. It was like they couldn't see her either. "Ronan, what did you do?"

"Don't worry, they're perfectly fine," he said, buzzing over to table and landing near her plate. "I've just woven them a little time suspension spell. You can go and do what you need to do, and while you're gone, I'll take care of your chores. The minute you return, the spell will be broken, you're chores will be done, and no one's the wiser."

"A time suspension spell?"

"One of the many things you'll get to learn, if you ever

leave!" he said impatiently.

"Okay, okay!" she said, getting up from the table. "Boy, you've got a short fuse -- no pun intended."

"Human humor," he mused. "Oh how have I lived for 23,175 years without it? Farewell, cailin," he said turning his back and getting to work.

Sarah Grace just headed for the front door, but had no idea where she should be going. She ran toward the tree, expecting Fiona to be there, but as she got closer and the fairy didn't appear, she began to wonder. Sarah Grace walked around the tree in a circle and saw nothing.

"Fiona?" she called, looking past the farm into the woods. Twenty feet away, the hard brown ground disappeared into a thicket of scrub trees and bushes. Sarah Grace didn't think much about it, until she saw little puffs of crystallized smoke rising into the air. Sarah Grace immediately panicked. Fire could mean the death of a tree farm, but before she could run back to warn her parents....

"Sarah Grace, come on," Fiona called.

Sarah Grace broke through the high grass into a small clearing where Fiona was throwing handfuls of dust onto a pile of stones.

"What are you doing? You're gonna start a fire!"

"No such luck," the fairy said, apparently disgusted with her efforts. "One of those days I wasn't really paying attention."

"Paying attention to what?" Sarah Grace asked, sitting down on a large rock.

"My training. Don't look at me like that," she said, with a hand on her hip. "From what I can hear about you, you've nodded off in class a time or two, yourself."

As Sarah Grace indignantly chewed on that insult, she jumped as something materialized in her lap. It was a little blue pouch, much like the one Fiona carried, except bigger with a shoulder strap. Her initials, 'SG', were embroidered in gold thread.

"Go ahead, open it."

With great anticipation, she pealed back the flap and saw.....nothing. "It's empty," she said, disappointment written all over her little face.

"Of course, it's empty," Fiona said. "What would happen if you lost it, or left it behind? What if your brothers found it? That's the last thing you want."

"But if it's empty, what would they find?" Sarah Grace

wondered absentmindedly, looking into the pouch again. "I mean, where's my magic wand? Shouldn't I have some magic rocks or something?"

Fiona shook her head. "Let's approach this another way," she said slowly, taking a deep breath. She fluttered to within an inch of Sarah Grace's face, dropped down and put her hand over the girl's heart. "This is where your magic is." Then she rose to her forehead. "This is where your magic lies as well. Without these -- your heart and your head -- your power means nothing. You'll never give it wings. You'll never give it life."

Her brow wrinkled. She put a hand to her heart, then scratched her head. "But Fiona, how does it work?"

"Concentration, mostly," the fairy explained. "Watch." Fiona moved over to a blue lumbago, that had yet to bloom, with its small periwinkle flowers. She gazed at the plant, and a serenity Sarah Grace had never seen in the little creature was evident. The plant shivered as if awakened by a sudden loud sound, and its flowers began to open.

Sarah Grace didn't know what she'd shut first; her eyes or her mouth. "How did you do that?" she asked in awe.

"Before you leave me today, you'll know."

Queen Nivia was pleased. The Sixteenth Order of the Fae Council had been rumbling ever since Fiona had gone in search of her cailin, and Nivia had had her misgivings as well. Fiona could be lazy and headstrong, but she was highly intelligent with sharp intuition. The only thing holding her back was the past.

It happened sometimes in her world. Though their ties with humans were primarily for self preservation, the lines were sometimes blurred, and a very real emotion like disappointment could muddy the waters.

"My Queen?"

Nivia closed her flower ball. "Yes?"

A Grogoch put a tray of refreshment on a small table next to the Queen's desk. Then he bowed and retreated.

It was a pleasing array of nectar juice, candied buds and leaf salad. Fairies didn't need much sustenance, but Nivia liked to indulge herself every once in a while. Sampling the delicate morsels, she called on her flower ball again. As the haze cleared, she could see the courtyard of the school Sarah Grace attended. There were no children on the campus, but Nivia saw someone she instantly recognized.

Mother Superior was nervous, and with good reason. Her goal

seemed attainable, but she was beginning to question the events of the past few days. She was a nun, a bride of Christ, and she'd fallen under the spell of a strange man, taken gifts from him, and was probably endangering the children around her to further her plans. Was there a vow she hadn't broken yet?

The girl would be better off, wouldn't she? What kind of existence was it for a child to move from home to home, never knowing a sense of belonging? Wendy would be getting a home when all was said and done, and she would be realizing the life she'd always wanted. Wasn't it what she wanted?

She moved from the desk in her office to the arched window which looked out into the reflection garden. It was a pretty spot. The children and their parents had worked tirelessly for several weekends planting flowers and placing stones for the rosary path. There was even a little seating area for outside programs, when the weather permitted. Mother Superior thought about the things that had been accomplished in her tenure here; a tenure, which for one reason or another, would probably end soon. The school had expanded to more than four hundred students. The church itself had been given a new life and the faithful had returned. The parish was successful, if one could say that about a church. Why couldn't she be happy with that?

The knock at the door made her jump. She took a moment to compose herself. "Yes, come in."

Father Francis swung the door wide because he was not alone. A pleasant looking couple moved past him into Mother Superior's office. They looked to be in their mid thirties. The man wore a brown suit, had a mustache and was balding slightly on top. The woman was of medium build, had a short afro and wore a pale blue shirt dress. They both had pleasing smiles.

"Mother Superior," Father Francis began, "let me introduce Mr. and Mrs. Jackson. They're very interested in adopting one of the children."

Mother Superior clutched at her heart and took a moment to find her voice. "It's very nice to meet you," she said as calmly as she could. "Which of our children interests you?"

"Wendy," Father Francis answered.

"W-Wendy," she responded slowly. "I see. Well, would you please have a seat and we'll discuss this?"

"Try just one more time, Sarah Grace," Fiona moaned, slumped over a log, her arm across her face. The plea had really been half-hearted. She'd been saying 'one more time' all afternoon. Fiona was tired, and her cailin was despondent.

"I can't do it, Fiona," she insisted, her little blue pouch long since discarded. She sat cross-legged on the ground in front of a rose bud, and try as she might, she could not make it open and bloom.

"You just have to focus your energy," Fiona reminded her.

Sarah Grace's shoulders slumped as she raised her eyes to the sky. After a final sigh, she uncrossed her legs and stood up, heading toward her house.

"Let me show you one more time," Fiona pressed.

"No!" the child screamed, turning on her heel and stomping back toward the fairy. "You've shown me a hundred times. Look around you," she said, holding out her arms. "Every flower around here has bloomed except the one in front of me. I just can't do it, Fiona. I can't! I can't!" And then the tears came; quiet, but steady.

Fiona sat up, and watched Sarah Grace. She fluttered over to the child and watched the water on her dusty cheeks. Touching the tears with gentle fingers, she could only wonder. She tasted the water. "It's salty," she proclaimed. "I know what tears are, but I didn't know they were salty."

Sarah Grace dragged a fist under her eyes to remove the

humiliating reminder of her failure. "I guess you were wrong about me," she said sniffling and clearing her throat. "I guess I'm not the right kid."

"Of course you're the right kid. Did you think this was going to happen overnight? It's taken me two thousand years to become a teacher, and to be frank, I could use a refresher course on a couple of things."

Sarah Grace looked at her with watery eyes and an arched eyebrow.

"Okay, more than a couple," she giggled. "But Sarah Grace, you can't give up. There's too much at stake."

Taking a moment to clear her mind, Sarah Grace looked back at her house, then at Fiona. Resolute, she walked back to the flower she'd been trying to open and knelt before it. She took a deep breath and closed her eyes. '*Heart and head,' she chanted in her mind, 'heart and head. Put all my power into making this flower beautiful.''* And she felt it. A tingling sensation shot up her spine and all at once she felt hot and cold while perspiration broke out on her brow. She was shaking as she opened her eyes. And the flower was opening!!!

Sarah Grace sat up on her knees with her small hands balled

into fists, doing everything she could to maintain her focus. She could feel her heart beating in her ears and it felt like a herd of mustangs was racing through her body. The flower continued to open. The petals were blood red and outlined with yellow. As the smallest petals unfolded and the center was exposed, there was a burst of gold dust. And for the first time in a few minutes, Sarah Grace exhaled.

"Yes!!!!" Fiona exclaimed, zipping into the air. "I knew you could do it! High five," she cried raising her hand.

Sarah Grace gave her one of those looks again. "High five?"

"Yeah. I saw it on that box in your living room. You know, the BV."

"You mean 'TV'," Sarah Grace laughed, slapping the fairy's offered hand.

"Look in your pouch, Sarah Grace," she instructed.

She'd almost forgotten about it, seeing the blue pouch discarded on the ground near her feet. She picked it up and it was noticeably heavier. Putting her hand in, she pulled out a red gemstone. "Is this a ruby?" she gasped.

Fiona nodded. "Every time you learn a new skill, you're

rewarded with a stone. In our world, they're very valuable."

"In ours, too. What do you do with them?"

"We trade them. Sometimes for other things, sometimes just to get other stones we like. They give us energy. The more stones you get, the easier it is to do the magic."

"Wow. How many stones can I earn?"

"No one really knows. You never stop learning, so you never stop earning."

"Do you have lots of stones?"

"Well, I'd have more if I didn't like to shop."

"Shop?" Sarah Grace asked, surprised. "Is there a mall in that tree?"

"Well, not exactly," Fiona laughed. "I like pretty colors on my wings. I trade with the Grogochs and they paint new colors on for me all the time. Queen Nivia doesn't always approve. She says I'm being frivolous."

"She sounds like my Mom," the girl laughed briefly, then stopped herself. "Uh, oh. My family! How long have we been out here?"

"I don't know," Fiona admitted.

"I've gotta get back!"

"Sarah Grace, wait," Fiona called to the girl's back.

"What is it?"

"Guard your pouch."

"From who?"

Fiona fluttered closer. "From everyone. To ordinary humans, it appears to be an empty pouch. But to your enemies, your fairy enemies, what's in the pouch is visible. Remember, it's one source of your magic. If it's lost, you're almost defenseless."

Chapter 6

"Sarah Grace! Sarah Grace!" Wendy called running across the schoolyard on Monday morning. In her excitement, she dropped her pencil case and the gold number two pencils spilled out all over the walkway.

Sarah Grace ran over to her friend to help. "What are you so excited about?"

"You'll never guess, you'll never guess," she challenged, almost on the brink of tears and laughter all at once.

"I'm sure I can't," she said, putting the last pencil in the box and closing it. She handed it to Wendy as they stood up.

"Sarah Grace, someone wants to adopt me! Can you believe it? Someone wants to adopt me. Me! And I'm an older kid."

Sarah Grace didn't know what to feel. On one hand, she was thrilled at the prospect. Wendy deserved a family. But on the other hand….. "You're not going to move away, are you?"

"Oh no; that's the best part." she said, grabbing her best friend's arm and propelling her toward their first class. "They live nearby. I haven't met them yet, but Mother Superior says they're really nice, and that I'm just the kind of daughter they want."

Sarah Grace wanted to be happy for her friend. But, anything to do with Mother Superior now gave her pause. Her 'guardian' had already betrayed her. Should Sarah Grace trust her to do right by her friend?

"Sarah Grace, what's wrong?" Wendy asked, all the excitement fading from her face. "Aren't you happy for me?"

"You know I am. This is what you've always wanted. I want you to be happy."

"Aaaarrrrrgggggghhhh!"

The pencil case dropped again as both girls jumped and screamed at the same time. Sarah Grace was so mad she was ready to scream once more. "What do you want, Devon?" she shouted. She'd have punched him, but that was the quickest way to after-school detention.

"What are all the smiles about?" he giggled impishly, bending down to help pick up the pencils.

"Not that it's any of your business," Wendy began, "but, someone wants to adopt me." She grabbed the last of the pencils, closed the case, and slipped it into her book bag.

Devon was actually silenced by the news. "Really?"

"What's the matter?" Sarah Grace asked. "Don't you think Wendy deserves a family?"

Devon shrugged a shoulder. "Why not? If a family can put up with you, Wendy should be a cake walk!"

The boy took off just as Sarah Grace balled up her fist.

"Don't even think about it," Wendy warned. "I need your help on the next spelling test. How can I get it if you're grounded?"

"What a butthead," she muttered under her breath. How in the world could her grandmother believe this boy liked her? Sarah Grace could barely stand to be in the same room with him.

The girls walked under the archway separating the church from the school. Sarah Grace gazed up and saw Mother Superior looking down from the balcony on the second floor landing. The looks they exchanged were cold and nondescript. It saddened her. The nun was different now. A couple of years ago, things had been different. Mother Superior had never been what you'd call an overly friendly woman, but she at least seemed to enjoy her students. Lately, she seemed distant and barely tolerant of her young charges, and it had only just occurred to Sarah Grace that the nun had taken an unusual interest in Wendy.

She met them just past the archway. "Good morning, girls," she called.

"Oh, good morning, Mother Superior," Wendy called happily, running into the woman's arms.

Sarah Grace didn't want to get any closer, but was careful not to show any disrespect.

"When can I meet them?" Wendy asked, barely able to contain her excitement. "They haven't changed their minds, have they?"

"Of course not," she said through a smile that didn't quite reach her eyes. "They may be by after lunch. They're very anxious to meet you, as well." Mother Superior looked at Sarah Grace. "I'm sure Wendy's told you her good news."

"Yes, she has."

"I'm sure you're happy for her."

Sarah Grace only nodded. She truly disliked adults who were sure about what she felt. "Yes, Mother Superior. It would be great if Wendy could have adults in her life she can always count on."

The woman's head snapped upwards, and she was met with

the defiant eyes of an adolescent girl who suddenly seemed older than her years.

"We'd better get to class," Sarah Grace said, taking Wendy's hand and pulling her away. "We sure don't want to be late."

Mother Superior nodded, dismissing them.

Watching the girls go, the nun felt uneasy. She'd always found Sarah Grace Littleton challenging in a way that other children wouldn't dare attempt. She seemed to have a knack for pointed comments with a double-edged meaning. She'd have to watch her more closely. Sarah Grace could easily disrupt her plans, and that was not an option.

"Mother Superior?" Sister Mary Agnes appeared at her side with a large envelope. "This just arrived for you and I thought it looked important."

"Thank you, sister," she said taking the envelope.

"Oh, is it true about little Wendy? She's to be adopted?"

"Well, we're still in the early stages. She'll meet the couple today. If they like each other, we'll proceed from there. "

Sister Mary Agnes put her hands together and shook her head. "You don't know how I've been praying for a home for that little girl. It's so hard for the older children, and she seems more eager than others to have a family connection. Do we know much about her birth family?"

"She came into the foster care system when she was only five. I've never met her natural parents, or any member of the family."

"How odd," the sister said mournfully. "You'd think the child would have at least one family member concerned with what happens to her."

"Well, Wendy has had an unfortunate beginning, but hopefully she can have a brighter future. If you'll excuse me, Sister," Mother Superior said, moving into her office.

A lone envelope was on her desk. The initial 'B' was scrawled across the front of the envelope in bold black script. Of course, she knew it was from him. She sat down and opened the envelope slowly, but her heart was already racing.

"I trust our plans are proceeding as expected. I hope to hear from you soon. How is our little Wendy?"

Mother Superior quickly put the note and envelope through the paper shredder under her desk. She had to be careful about any contact and could leave no trace of her relationship with her new master. She was ashamed of herself, but not for the reasons others might have believed. She wasn't ashamed that she'd broken most of her vows. She was ashamed of her awe of his power, and how much she wanted it for herself.

Sarah Grace shoved her book bag into her locker and shut the metal door a little louder than she'd meant to, as evidenced by all the children looking her way. Trying to cover, she pretended the locker was stuck and pulled it open again.

"What are you so cranky about?" Fiona asked.

Sarah Grace gasped and jumped back. "You scared me to death!"

"You're right," Ronan said to Fiona, climbing to the top of her book pile and taking off his hat. "She is in a foul mood."

"What do you know about my mood?" she snapped, whispering so that the students passing her in the hall wouldn't hear.

"It's her job to know how her cailin is feeling," Ronan explained. "If she didn't, how would she know how to help you?"

"And you've been giving off negative vibes all day," Fiona

said. "You have to be better at hiding your emotions, or you may put yourself at risk."

"It's hard for me to be nice to someone who's out to hurt me," Sarah Grace complained. "Something's going on, too. I'm worried about Wendy. Something's not right about this adoption, and I don't know what it is."

"Sarah Grace?" came a masculine voice from behind her.

She closed her locker and turned slowly. "Oh hello, Father Francis."

"Were you speaking to someone?" he asked, looking past her shoulder.

"Oh no," she lied, "I was just trying to memorize some history facts. You know how Sister Angelica is."

"Ah yes. She loves pop quizzes," he smiled. "May I walk with you to the lunch room?"

"Sure," she said, wondering why she was rating this extra attention. Sarah Grace didn't know much about this priest, except that some in the parish thought he was a little too young. This was actually the first time she'd ever spoken to him face to face.

"It's wonderful about Wendy, isn't it?"

"I guess so."

"Wouldn't you like to see her be adopted?" he asked, concern in his voice.

"If they're the right people and she'll be happy. I want her to be happy."

"But you have reservations."

That was a big word, she thought to herself. They reached the door of the cafeteria and the unmistakable aroma of watered down milk and pressed hamburger assaulted her senses.

"Smells like mystery meat to me," he said.

Sarah Grace had to giggle.

"With a side order of limp salad and day old mashed potatoes."

She laughed again. For a priest, he was kind of funny.

At that moment, Wendy came running up to her. "Come on, Sarah Grace, let's get our lunch," she said excitedly, taking her friend's hand. "I get to meet them after lunch. Will you come with me?"

"I don't know, Wendy," she admitted, uncertainly. If Mother Superior was part of that meeting, Sarah Grace wasn't sure she'd be invited.

Father Francis put his hand on her back and Sarah Grace jumped. A strange force seemed to radiate from the area where his hand lay. Sarah Grace looked over her shoulder, but avoided making eye contact with the priest. As Wendy pulled her away and the contact was broken, there was a cooling effect and then the strange sensation was gone. Father Francis said good-bye and walked away.

Sarah Grace took a deep breath and shyly looked in his direction as he left the lunchroom.

Wendy barely maintained any sense of composure during lunch, and standing outside Mother Superior's office door waiting to go in, she was close to coming unglued. Sarah Grace stood next to her, holding her hand, and putting an arm around her shoulder, but nothing would keep Wendy still.

She smoothed herself and the front of her skirt for the fiftieth time, and looked to her best friend for approval. Sarah Grace would nod. Wendy was so excited, and she didn't want to share her doubts.

Both girls jumped as the heavy door creaked open. "Wendy," Mother Superior smiled. But the smile dipped when she saw Sarah Grace holding the girl's hand. "And Sarah Grace," she said, with a terse nod of her head. "If you'll excuse us, please. There are some people I'd like Wendy to meet."

"Can't Sarah Grace come with me, Mother Superior? She wants to meet them, too."

"I don't think that would be a good idea at this time, Wendy," the woman told her soothingly. "It's important you make this first meeting with your prospective parents alone," she emphasized. Looking back at Sarah Grace, the edge already back in her demeanor, "Sarah Grace can meet them another time."

She'd seen that look before. It was meant to squelch any argument and of course, Sarah Grace knew it well.

"You'd better go on to class now and Wendy will join you soon."

Sarah Grace squeezed Wendy's hand with the reassurance only a best friend could provide, then let it go and walked down the hall.

The meeting must have gone well, because Wendy was bubbling over with excitement about every little detail. Their last name was Kingston. The lady had worn a yellow dress with little white flowers. The man wore a blue tie and asked her if she like to read, because he liked to read. The couple sat on the sofa, and she got to sit in between them, just like a real daughter. They were coming back in a few days to see her again, and they'd bring a picture of their house.

"Mother Superior said that I might even get to go to their house for the weekend for a trial visit."

"A trial visit?" Sarah Grace asked as the yellow school bus neared her stop. Wendy's foster family gave her permission to go home with her today and do homework.

"Yeah. That means we spend the weekend together, and if we all get along okay, then maybe they'll adopt me."

Sarah Grace was doing her best to be upbeat, but something about this didn't sit well with her. She'd give anything for Wendy to have a permanent family like hers, but there was something about the way Mother Superior was acting which gave her pause.

"Hi, Momma, hi Grammy," she said, as they came through the front door. At this time of day, her mother and grandmother were usually in the kitchen beginning preparations for dinner.

"Hey, Bumblebee," Grammy greeted both girls, her arms thrown wide enough to give them both a hug at the same time.

"Hi, Mrs. Littleton," said Wendy. "Did Sarah Grace tell you?"

"Tell me what?" the woman asked, looking up from the dinner she was preparing.

Sarah Grace listened as Wendy told her mother all the news, until she was distracted by noises coming from her bedroom. She was down the hall in seconds, then in front of her door. "What do you think you're doing?" she cried.

Jonathan and Brucie quickly shut dresser drawers and spun around. "Nothing," they parroted in unison.

"You're snooping!"

"No, we're not," Brucie insisted quietly, not wanting to bring his mother down the hall.

"Then, what?"

"We just want to know what's been going on with you lately," Jonathan said.

"Nothing's been going on with me lately," she snapped. "I can't believe you two were snooping in my room! Just wait."

"Wait for what?" Brucie asked. "You gonna run to Daddy? I don't think so. Something's going on. And if you don't want to tell us, you sure don't want to tell the folks."

"Bruce," Jonathan scolded, "you don't have to make it sound like that. Look Sis, we're not just trying to be pains. You've just looked a little sad lately. Can we help?"

Sarah Grace was almost ashamed. Her brothers could certainly be annoying, but they'd always been protective of her. She couldn't tell them what was really going on, but…."I've just been stressed out about Wendy."

"Why?" Brucie asked.

"There's a couple interested in adopting her."

"Well, that's good, isn't it?" Jonathan questioned with a wrinkled brow. "Or, are you worried about losing your friend?"

Even if she wasn't telling them the whole truth, that was certainly a concern she could respond to. "Yes."

Sarah Grace spied her blue pouch sitting on her desk where she'd left it. It looked flat and empty, and her brothers clearly had no idea what was in it, just as Fiona had said.

"Boys," Momma called, "I need your help."

"Coming, Momma," Jonathan called. Looking back at his little sister, he said, "Look small fry, if you need us…"

"Yeah, I know. I'm sorry I yelled at you."

On the way out, Brucie gave her a brotherly shove and laughed.

"Jerk," she whispered as they left. And slobs. They weren't even good snoops, she thought, putting the things on her dresser back in order.

"And you think I'm particular," came her grandmother's voice from the door. "They didn't mean any harm, you know. You have been acting strangely, lately." Grammy walked in and closed the door.

"Where's Wendy?" asked Sarah Grace.

"Helping your Momma with the cookies. Talk about a child starved for mothering," she said quietly, shaking her head as she moved toward her granddaughter.

Sarah Grace continued to straighten and put away her things. The pouch was deftly shoved into her sock drawer and she turned around to face her grandmother. The look she saw on the woman's face brought some concern, but she didn't know what she should be concerned about. "Did you want something, Grammy?"

"I don't think it's me that you should be asking that question."

More riddles. "What do you mean?" "Made any new friends lately?" she asked, her head cocked to one side.

"Wendy's my best friend, you know that. What other friends do I need?"

"You're only eleven years old, Sarah Grace," Grammy chuckled. "Wendy won't be the only friend you'll ever have. I meant new friends, different friends."

Sarah Grace could see that Grammy was trying to pull some kind of answer out of her, but on her life, she couldn't tell what.

Grammy stepped forward and put her small hands to Sarah Grace's cheeks. "You know, the universe is different things to different people. Some of us will end up leading lives we never thought we would. I just think you're one of those people." After kissing the girl on her forehead, she simply turned and left. No look over her should, no clarification of her last statement.

Sarah Grace's brow wrinkled and her eyes drew together. Is it possible Grammy knew about Fiona? After half a second of consideration, she just shook her head. "No."

"You're doing really well, Sarah Grace," Fiona said. She watched as the girl changed the colors of a flower from blue to green, then back to blue again. They'd been working steadily over the last couple of weeks, and Sarah Grace's powers were increasing every day. The only thing she was having a problem with, was actually seeing other members of the fairy world who were not obvious. Fairies didn't have this ability, which is why they had to depend on their cailins. Sarah Grace was blocking it, and Fiona wasn't sure why.

The color transformation was over, and Sarah Grace opened her eyes, pleased with her efforts. "What's next?"

"You could be asking that question for the rest of your natural life," Fiona laughed. "There's always a lesson to be learned." The fairy fluttered over to a rock next to Sarah Grace and sat down. "I'll bet your pouch is pretty heavy now."

"Yeah," Sarah Grace agreed, lifting it and feeling its weight. "I'll bet this is worth a lot of money, too."

"Probably."

"Is money worth a lot in that tree?" she asked, motioning

behind her.

"No," Fiona answered, thoughtfully, "but the jewels are. Some would do anything for them."

"Like who?"

"She'll never answer that question," Ronan said, appearing out of the blue. He dusted himself off, but that did nothing to disinfect him.

"Maybe you should stand there," Sarah Grace directed, pointing to a spot to her left. "It's downwind."

"Do I offend?" he asked sarcastically.

"Every day of your life," Fiona grumbled.

"Someone betrayed you once, didn't they, Fiona?" Sarah Grace asked.

"Smart girl," Ronan said slyly.

Fiona averted her eyes and was not forthcoming. It had been centuries ago, and she didn't like to think about it.

"Was it your guardian?"

"Fairies don't have guardians," she sighed. "Sometimes I wish they did. She was a friend, or at least I thought she was my friend."

"Orva was no one's friend," Ronan said, "but you couldn't see that. No matter what anyone told you."

"What did she do?" Sarah Grace asked, now intrigued.

Fiona was still silent, obviously deeply affected by whatever had happened.

Ronan had no such problem. "She managed to steal all of Fiona's gems, rendering her almost powerless. By the time Fiona had gotten her strength back and was able to defend herself, Orva was gone, never to be heard from again. Her name is rarely spoken in our world. Queen Nivia all but forbids it. We don't have many traitors, and in my many years, Orva is the only one I've known personally."

Sarah Grace watched Fiona carefully. Her small shoulders were slumped, and her gaze was distant. "You must have loved her a lot," she observed, trying to comfort.

Just that quickly, Fiona turned, her eyes glittering like glass, fluttering defiantly above the two. "We don't love!" And with that she was gone.

Sarah Grace looked to Ronan for an explanation.

"Fairies are created in groups, what we like to call 'crystal pods'. For whatever reason, no one knows why, only Fiona and Orva survived their pod. They grew up together, learned together, had adventures together. They were like you and Wendy, I suppose. When Orva betrayed her, Fiona lost interest in everything. That is of course, until you came along," Ronan completed with his trademark wink, and was gone a second later.

Sarah Grace picked up the gem pouch. It was very heavy. She'd never really counted, but there must be at least fifty or sixty gems inside. Growing up with humans had taught her at least one thing. If it was valuable, it was worth stealing. And some didn't care what they had to do to get it.

Chapter 7

Ronan flew off in pursuit of Fiona. When she was upset like this, there was only one place in which she was comfortable. Gaining entrance to the tree, he traveled through the many levels of their world, and came to an oasis, which mimicked a rain forest. Water was spilling in gentle ripples from a rock formation high above the floor of a pond, which was encircled by flagstones and outgrowths of ferns and brightly colored flowers. And that's where he found her. Sitting on a slick stone, cooling her feet in the water.

"You know," he began, bouncing on the stones behind her for maximum annoyance, "for someone who doesn't love, you reacted pretty strongly to a long past memory."

Fiona barely acknowledged his presence, but recognized Ronan in this mood. He'd be like a fly in her face until she agreed with him or had a knock-down-drag-out fight instead. "Ronan, if you've ever felt any affection for me, or anything not buried thirty feet underground and smelling like garbage, you'll leave me in peace."

"You know I'm not wired that way, Fiona," he smirked.

She stood up in irritation, squeezing the water off her wings and noticing how the colors seemed to be fading just a bit. The Grogoch who'd painted them for her had told her not to get them wet for a fortnight and she'd forgotten. How fleeting their beauty had been, she wondered to herself -- as had been many other things in her existence.

"How long do you intend to sit here and pout?" Ronan poked.

"Until I choose not to pout anymore," she said.

"You can't afford the luxury," Ronan reminded her. "Summer Solstice is upon us in a short time, and your cailin still cannot discern a member of the Fae world from normal human beings. She'll be of no use to us."

"Ronan is correct, Fiona," came a lilting voice from behind them.

It was a very distinct voice. They both turned and bowed. Nivia received the honor with little notice, as she floated above to perch on a branch near the water.

"I hadn't expected to see you this soon. Are you hiding again, my dear?"

"No, Your Highness. I'm just taking a small respite. Working with my cailin is sometimes challenging."

"How is the child progressing?"

"Very well, Majesty."

Ronan cleared his throat.

"But….?" Nivia prompted.

Fiona looked at Ronan and wished she had the nerve to cut out his tongue. "She does appear to have a problem identifying the Fae."

"Isn't that the main purpose of her life?"

"Yes, Highness, but she resists."

"Does she resist, Fiona? Or perhaps you've failed to impart to her exactly how it is done?"

Fiona looked up and she didn't know if she should be indignant or contrite.

"Do you think this child was chosen randomly; that she had no celestial link to your life, Fiona?" Nivia asked.

"Your Highness," Fiona sputtered.

"Or perhaps you think because you could not see evil, you cannot teach her to see evil. Yours was simply a failing of youth, and a question of faith. So is hers. You are now in the unique position of being able to impart that wisdom."

Fiona's demeanor had gone from one of defiance to one of confusion. She didn't know how to help Sarah Grace on this one, and it wasn't because she'd missed a lesson or two. The floodgates of emotion she'd felt, due to Orva's betrayal had been easily masked with pretty colors. She couldn't teach Sarah Grace about the pain of betrayal, because it meant having to let it in again, and understanding it herself.

"Your thoughts betray you, Fiona," Queen Nivia said, the clarity in her eyes. "You have a task to complete. I need not remind you of its importance."

Fiona squared her shoulders then bowed low. "Yes, Your Highness."

Sarah Grace pulled up the comforter on her bed and placed her pillows on top. She went over to her desk to grab her book bag for school, and saw her blue pouch sitting on top of her books. Sarah Grace remembered what Fiona had told her. *Guard your pouch. Your enemies can see what's inside.* Where were my enemies, she wondered? Sarah Grace grabbed the pouch and stuffed it into her book bag. She decided you could never too careful.

The rest of the family was already at the table for breakfast. As usual, Brucie and Jonathan were fighting over who'd gotten more pancakes, Daddy was eating as he read the newspaper, and Momma was going over her schedule, as she sipped at coffee and nibbled at toast.

"Good morning," she said, sitting down and reaching for a pancake with her fork.

Salutations were mumbled, but everyone remained behind that invisible shield, which was always present on Mondays. They were tired from the weekend, and no one was willing to greet another workweek. Sarah Grace had two major tests in her conventional world, and goodness knew how many in her fantasy world. She hadn't seen Fiona since their last meeting, and she was truly worried she'd offended her new friend -- if that's what she could call Fiona. She wasn't exactly like Wendy, but you couldn't exactly call Fiona a simple acquaintance.

"Sarah Grace," her mother called to her gently.

"Yes, Momma?" She was greeted by the stares of her entire family, and at first she didn't know why.

"Do you always take a cup of syrup on your pancake?" Daddy asked.

Sarah Grace abruptly righted the bottle and used a spoon to ladle the spilled syrup back onto her plate. "Sorry."

"Is everything all right?" Momma asked.

"You were in a different world," said Daddy.

"She's worried," Brucie said in between bites.

"About Wendy getting adopted," Jonathan added.

"Well, sweetheart, why would you be worried about that?" her mother wondered. "According to Wendy, they're a very nice couple and they live nearby."

"I know," she admitted.

"Are you thinking she won't have much time for you after she's been adopted?" her father asked.

Sarah Grace just nodded her head. What else could she say?

"It probably will be like that at first," her father continued. "You know how it is, when you get a new book or a new toy. It's all you can think about and play with for a long time. But then, those familiar things make their way back into your life," he said with a wink and a smile. "You just give Wendy some time."

"Your father's right, Sarah Grace," Velvet Littleton agreed.

"You just do what you've always done for your best friend. Be there if she needs you. There'll be a lot of uncertainty those for her those first few days and weeks, and she'll need your shoulder to lean on."

She'd gone quiet for a moment when something suddenly occurred to her. "Where's Grammy?"

"Still in bed," her mother answered. "She wasn't feeling well this morning."

"Is she okay?" Brucie asked, all the children now immediately concerned.

"Yes," their father assured them. "The doctor just gave her a new medication and it's making her a little tired."

"A new medication for what?" Jonathan asked.

"Her cholesterol's a little high, but it's nothing to be worried about," said Momma.

"What's cholesterol?" Sarah Grace wondered aloud. "You mean that yellow stuff you put in my hair sometimes?"

Velvet laughed softly to herself, but really offered no explanation; just additional assurances that Grammy was fine, and sent them off to school.

As the overly warm school bus jostled along the road leading away from her home, she thought to herself that her parents were probably right. She should put her feelings aside and support her friend. So, Sarah Grace pasted a smile on her face as Wendy walked down the aisle and sat down.

"Hi, Sarah Grace," she chirped. "I saw them this weekend."

"Them?"

"Yeah; my new parents."

"Oh, I didn't know it was official yet."

"Well, not yet," she admitted, bowing her head. "The three of us are all getting along really well. They took me to the mall and we got ice cream. They even took me to the bedding department and asked me what kinds of things I would like in my very own bedroom. Do you think they're decorating it now?"

"Maybe," Sarah Grace offered, trying to sound upbeat. Other children currently in foster care from their school had been adopted, and the children always shared the details in the run-up to the official act. She couldn't recall any couple getting as much access to the children as Wendy was experiencing, though. Regardless, she took her friend's hand and squeezed it. "I'm glad you're happy, Wendy."

The bus ground to a squeaky halt in front of the school and fresh air flooded in, as the narrow double doors flipped open. Sarah Grace and Wendy usually sat in the back and let the rowdier children exit first.

"Did you study for the test?" Wendy asked.

"Which one?" Sarah Grace grimaced.

"Both, I guess. I'm pretty good on the social studies, but I'm still not sure about science."

"Just remember the stuff we did in the workbook. Sister Angelica usually takes her questions from there." "Good idea. I want to have really good grades. They'll probably want a kid who's smart."

Sarah Grace didn't comment on that. Who wouldn't want a girl like Wendy, even if she did mostly make B's and C's. She was a great friend and a really nice girl.

"Good morning, girls," Mother Superior greeted them at the entrance to their class.

"Good morning," they said; though Wendy's voice definitely held more welcome than Sarah Grace's.

"Did you have a good weekend?"

"Oh yes," Wendy spoke up quickly. "I had a wonderful time with Mr. and Mrs. Kingston."

Mother Superior laughed. "I know. I've already spoken with them this morning, and they said you were delightful."

"They did?" she asked excitedly.

"Of course."

"Does that mean they'll adopt me?"

Mother Superior made a point of looking at Sarah Grace with the most insincere smile she could conjure. "The prospects look very good, Wendy."

"What a hag," Fiona commented, peering over a light fixture in the lunchroom. She and Ronan had been privy to the exchange between Mother Superior and the girls, and her dislike of the fallen guardian had reached an all-time high. Like it or not, she did harbor some genuine affection for Sarah Grace, and didn't enjoy watching someone intentionally inflict discomfort on her. "Whoever chose her chose well," she said with disdain. "You don't get that nasty overnight."

"True," Ronan agreed. "She does seem to have an innate talent for twisting the knife slowly. It would serve her right if I dropped some poison ivy leaves down her habit."

"Ronan," Fiona scolded, "while I admire your ingenuity; not now. I don't need an itchy rash complicating matters."

His chunky shoulders slumped and he frowned.

"Okay," she conceded, "but not until we figure out who the other bad guys are."

He brightened immediately, then disappeared. Ronan was still a mystery to Fiona. While he was a companion, he could hardly be called a friend. He seemed to barely tolerate the existence of others, as if they were only a hindrance to whatever it was he was looking for. He was obedient to the Queen, but was completely unimpressed with Fae society.

Sarah Grace had been a good student so far. She understood the spells for changing matter, time suspension, and what it took to destroy an enemy. But, none of these spells would mean very much if she couldn't identify who that enemy was. As Fiona observed her with Mother Superior, she could tell Sarah Grace's powers of identification were improving. She could sense something unsettling about her friend's possible adoption, and Fiona was sure it had something to do with whoever had infiltrated Sarah Grace's guardian.

Queen Nivia was right. Fiona was having trouble teaching Sarah Grace to open herself to the evil that lay beyond and in front of her. It was painful. She remembered. It was hard to teach someone to go looking for that sort of grief. Fiona tried to remember what it had been like with Orva, a fairy who'd been the whole world to her. She'd been completely open to every thought, every sense, and every adventure.

Fiona was always happy when Orva was around. Always happy. Always happy! Happy versus sad. Content versus discontent. Open versus closed. Positive versus negative. Sarah Grace's negative feelings surrounding Mother Superior were making it nearly impossible for her to see the enemy. That was it!

The nun had departed, and the girls were now sitting at a table eating their lunch. From what Fiona could see of human food, she'd take the nectar of flowers and rose petal snacks any day. How they could eat the flesh of animals was beyond her. That little boy Devon must have found it particularly distasteful, because he was tossing bits of it across the room to another boy. He was immediately collared by one of the sisters and escorted out of the cafeteria.

Sarah Grace was opening her milk when she noticed Father Francis, walking between the portable tables filled with students and half eaten lunches. Though she rarely enjoyed the lunches, she was sometimes distressed by the amount of food that was wasted. Having someone like Wendy for a friend could really reshape your perspective on things. Sarah Grace was sure she'd be a much more selfish person, had it not been for someone with Wendy's experiences.

Wendy usually ate everything on her plate. Her mother told her once, it was probably because Wendy was never really sure when she would get her next meal. Apparently, her upbringing had meant many hunger-filled nights at the hands of her neglectful mother. Sarah Grace looked at her friend and smiled, but the tranquil feeling was short-lived. She suddenly felt nauseated and broke into a cold sweat. Her hands were shaking so uncontrollably that she had to set her milk down on the table.

"Sarah Grace?" Father Francis called to her.

But Sarah Grace could barely hear him. She was staring at the priest through some kind of befuddled haze, and his words seemed to bounce off every object in the room. He reached a hand toward her, but Sarah Grace was instantly repelled. In her attempt to get away, she fell off her seat and banged her head against the table behind her.

"Sarah Grace!!" Wendy shouted.

Her name was the last thing she heard before she was suffocated by darkness.

Chapter 8

"Don't be afraid, cailin," she heard the soft voice say, as she swam back to consciousness. "Let go of the anger, and you will see your enemy. Let go of the anger."

Sarah Grace's eyes fluttered open and she took a deep breath. Every sense now seemed to be heightened. The room was too bright, the smell of antiseptic too strong, and the hand patting hers, grating against her tingling skin. She sat up abruptly and the room was spinning again.

"Not too fast," crooned the school nurse, Sister Beatrice. "You've got a little bump on the back of your head."

A hand went to the spot and Sarah Grace winced. "What happened?" she asked breathlessly.

"Apparently you fell and hit your head in the lunchroom."

"I always knew the mystery meat would kill me one day," she joked, all be it weakly.

The sister smiled. "We haven't lost a student yet. Your parents are on their way. You're probably fine, but they should take you to see your family doctor, to be on the safe side." Sister Beatrice patted her hand again, then went to her desk to fill out the paperwork on this particular incident.

"Psst!"

By now, Sarah Grace knew how to be discreet when Fiona appeared. She only nodded at her fairy teacher hiding in her cupped hand.

"Don't be afraid."

"What really happened to me?" she wanted to know. Sarah Grace had never fainted in her life.

"Your powers are just getting stronger. When you first become aware of the Fae, you don't always know how to handle the sensation."

"The Fae?"

"Those from my world."

"I didn't feel that way when I met you."

"That's because I wanted you to see me. Your senses will become stronger now."

"I don't know how it happened."

"What were you thinking about when you started to feel strange?"

It took her a moment to recall what had happened before. "I was thinking about Wendy, and how she always eats everything on her plate, no matter how gross the rest of us think the cafeteria food is. I felt kind of selfish, because I complain sometimes about what I have to eat, but I've never gone hungry. She's so strong and I just, I just...."

"Love her?" Fiona filled in the words which are sometimes so hard for humans to say.

Sarah Grace lowered her eyes. "I guess so," she whispered shyly. Children rarely thought about the emotion unless they were talking about their own parents.

"Sarah Grace!"

Fiona made a quick exit as the Littletons rushed in to check on their daughter.

All told, it had been a long day. Once she'd been checked out of school, Sarah Grace was taken to her pediatrician. Dr. Miller was impressed with the little bump on her head, but said there'd be no lasting damage, short of a slight headache. Her parents took her home and put her to bed. Brucie and Jonathan were immediately forced into servitude, fetching and carrying for their little sister, since her parents would not allow her to move a muscle.

She'd had her dinner served on a tray in her bedroom, and once she assured her parents that she felt fine, they retired to their other responsibilities, and her brothers attended to their homework. Sarah Grace pulled a book from her desk, but Fiona jumped from the pages.

Sarah Grace gasped. "Are you trying to give me a heart attack!" she whispered forcefully.

"Sorry," the fairy apologized, flying upward to be on eye level. "I didn't get to finish when you were in the nurse's office. "Sarah Grace, who was around you when you started to feel funny?"

"Lots of people," she answered, shrugging her shoulders.

"Think Sarah Grace. Who was standing around you at the time?"

"Well," she began thoughtfully, "Wendy was eating with me, and our classmates, and…" There her voice and her expression froze.

"Who was it, Sarah Grace?"

She looked at the fairy. "It was Father Francis," she croaked, almost in tears with the admission. "I didn't feel bad until he came by me."

"Was it the first time?"

She shook her head, with new understanding. "Last week, he touched my back and I felt funny again. How can a priest make me feel like that?"

"Because he's probably not a priest," said Ronan, appearing next to Fiona.

"What?" Sarah Grace asked, now very confused.

"If you've actually identified your first Fae, he's probably a changeling."

"A changeling? What's that?"

"They can be enemies or they can be friends," said Ronan cryptically.

"They're the hired help," Fiona all but sneered, with an arched eyebrow. "Someone, probably a Droke…"

"A Droke?"

"Just think of a Droke as a bad fairy," Fiona explained.

"A very bad fairy," Ronan emphasized.

"Drokes want to control the fairy world, and they'll do anything to achieve that," Fiona continued. "A Droke is at the bottom of this mystery, believe me, and if Father Francis is a changeling, he was hired."

Sarah Grace swallowed hard. "So you're telling me there are more bad fairies out there and it's up to me to help you find them."

"Yes," Fiona nodded.

"But why, Fiona?" she asked. "Why are they here and what do they want?"

Fiona and Ronan looked at each other, and those looks worried Sarah Grace. There was obviously something grave at stake, and Fiona was probably looking for just the right words before she broke the news.

"Sarah Grace," she said slowly, every syllable measured, "Drokes are not immortals. Just like Ronan, they can live many thousands of years, but they will eventually cease to exist. To take over the Fae world, you have to be an immortal. For a mortal to become immortal, they need just one thing."

"What's that?" she asked, bracing her back against her headboard.

"The innocence of a child," Ronan told her.

"You mean me?"

Fiona shook her head.

Sarah Grace's mind started to race at that very moment. Did they mean her brothers? No, no, they were older and so far hadn't figured into the scenario. A child's innocence, a child's innocence? "Oh my, God," she moaned. "Not… not Wendy?"

Fiona and Ronan nodded.

Now, Sarah Grace really thought she was going to be sick. She swallowed hard, then threw her feet to the floor and started to pace. And all the time, Fiona and Ronan tried to explain to her why her best friend was in such danger. These Drokes were not just interested in taking over the fairy world, but all the worlds which worked with Queen Nivia to ensure tranquility in the universe. For some odd reason, they could not detect what she was, but she could see them, and that alone made her a dangerous adversary. Except for one thing, of course. They'd had thousands of years to learn their craft, and she'd only had a few weeks to learn hers. Sarah Grace wasn't crazy about the very steep learning curve she was being subjected to.

"Sarah Grace," Fiona called to her. "The Summer Solstice is soon."

They'd probably told her before, the importance of that date, but now for the life of her she couldn't remember its significance. Every new piece of information was darker and scarier than the last, and Sarah Grace didn't know if she could hear much more. She started off this day still entertaining a fantasy. It hadn't materialized yet, that she'd be called upon to save lives, specifically that of her best friend. Up until that moment, it had all still been some kind of fantastic game of collecting gems and crystals. ...The pouch!

Sarah Grace moved quickly to her book bag, undid the zipper and dumped out its contents. She could breathe again. The pouch was still there. Sarah Grace hugged it to her chest. She'd worried about her little stash of rubies and emeralds before, worried that they would fall into human hands. Now that an enemy was out there, an enemy which she would only sense but not recognize, those jewels were as precious to her as her own blood.

"Sarah Grace," Fiona called to her.

She put the pouch back into her book bag, then turned to the fairy and said simply, "I need tonight."

"You need tonight?" Fiona asked.

"You need tonight for what?" Ronan wondered.

"To say good-bye," she told them.

Ronan was confused, but it made perfect sense to Fiona. "We'll see you tomorrow," she said, and nodded as they departed.

Sarah Grace tucked the book bag under her bed; then, left her room. She traveled down the dimly lit hallway to the living room, where the soft glow of the television set seeped into every corner, with its flickering shadows. Her father was in his usual spot on the oversized sofa, with a beer on one side of the coffee table and his laptop and a stack of financial files on the other. This was when he did his paperwork, though it was a slow business when you were trying to watch a football game at the same time. Somehow, he made it work.

He was a little surprised when she sat down and curled up next to him. "Couldn't sleep?" he asked, leaning back and wrapping a meaty arm around her small shoulders.

She only shook her head.

"Are you feeling okay? Does your head hurt? Do I need to get your Momma?"

She could hear the panic rising in his voice. "No, Daddy, I'm fine," she assured him, curling closer. This was how they used to be, before she felt she was too big for this kind of closeness. This was the year she and Wendy had become more interested in nail polish and the latest designer jeans, than riding on the tractor and eating berries as they were being picked. She and her father had both felt the disconnect, but knew it was the natural order of things. His 'little girl' was beginning the slow process of slipping away from him. The process was usually completed on her wedding day, and if he was lucky, he'd get a little of it back when the grandchildren came along.

Sarah Grace felt like she wanted to cry, but knew she wouldn't be able to explain the reason why she was doing so. This was her last night to feel this kind of warmth and protection. Little did her father know that from now on, she would be protecting his world, as much as he believed he was protecting hers.

Fiona and Ronan watched from outside the living room window of the Littleton home as Sarah Grace sat wrapped in her father's embrace.

"How can they sit and watch that glowing box as much as they do?" Ronan wondered. "It's all pictures and noise."

"I don't think she's watching," Fiona told him, her voice wistful and her heart heavy. She felt she had a clue of what Sarah Grace was feeling right now. Every sorrowful feeling she'd ever owned surrounded Orva and that betrayal. Saying good-bye; feeling regret; facing a truth. Now Fiona truly understood why Sarah Grace had been chosen for her.

"What did she mean she needed tonight to say good-bye?" Ronan asked. "She doesn't need to go anywhere to do what she needs to do."

"She's not saying good-bye to her home, Ronan," Fiona told him. "She's saying good-bye to this life."

The next school day started off just like any other. Sarah Grace had breakfast with her family, grabbed her book bag and walked out the door. Before she even got to the bus stop, Fiona was on her shoulder.

"Think about the people you love, Sarah Grace," Fiona instructed. "Then your enemies will be revealed. Maintain your focus. Remember what the end result needs to be and you'll be fine."

"All right, Fiona," she said, her voice holding little emotion as the bus pulled up. "Catch you later."

Fiona was gone by the time she boarded the bus. As usual, she sat in the back and waited the next couple of stops for Wendy to board. Wendy was usually full of smiles at the sight of her best friend, but this morning Sarah Grace could see the anxiety in her eyes. She gave her a big smile, which immediately alleviated the distress.

"Are you okay?" Wendy asked.

"I'm fine," she assured the girl. "I just had a little headache, but it's gone now."

"You were the talk of the school yesterday," Wendy said, properly impressed.

There was nothing like a bump on the head to get the gossip mill going. That little bump had surely turned into a tumor and Sarah Grace probably only had a few months to live. She'd get a strange array of stares, whispers and outright divine prophecies because of that bump. If only they knew of the prophecy already being fulfilled.

They were already off the bus and through the entrance of the school when the feeling began to hit Sarah Grace. One of them was near. She took Wendy's hand and thought of her best friend. When Wendy smiled back, the feeling was stronger, but she controlled her reaction. It was like forcing yourself not to vomit when you really wanted to. The source of her discomfort was already before her.

"Good morning, girls," Father Francis greeted them. "Sarah Grace, I do hope you're feeling better."

"Much better, Father," she responded, trying to remember that he was only the hired help. Reducing him to that level rendered him much less threatening. But Sarah Grace also understood now, that he was small potatoes. There was something more sinister lurking in the shadows, and as she held onto her friend's hand, she was more determined now to unearth it.

"Sarah Grace," called Mother Superior. "I'm glad you felt well enough to return to school today."

"Thank you, Mother Superior," she said coolly, maintaining her composure. "We'd better get to class." She pulled Wendy along, not wanting to spend any more time with those two than was necessary. She'd gotten through her first meeting. She hadn't gotten sick. Sarah Grace was feeling better already.

Mother Superior watched them go, with a sense of uneasiness filling her heart. Sarah Grace Littleton used to be no more than an annoyance to her. She was getting the feeling that the little girl could actually become a hindrance to her plans. Her head jerked upward as the nine o'clock bell sounded. She might be late to her meeting, a meeting she was not looking forward to.

Her Master was becoming impatient. He didn't understand paperwork, red tape and social worker visits. She was already pushing this adoption as quickly as she could. If she was any more aggressive, she'd draw far too much attention.

Mother Superior reached her office, went in and closed the door. Leaning against it almost out of breath, the woman looked around the sparsely furnished room and all her old resentments came to the surface. The room was essentially devoid of color. Not even the potted geranium on her desk provided her senses any relief. But, this had been her life. Little joy, and only brief moments of contentment. When she'd chosen this life, she'd been promised peace. It hadn't come.

"You're late," a voice hissed from behind her.

The woman almost fell to the floor, startled.

The room darkened almost immediately and all she could make out was the glow of two red points of light.

Chapter 9

"There, there, Mother Superior," he crooned. "There's no need to be concerned. After all, we're old friends." He extended a hand and without touching the frightened woman, willed her to her feet.

Mother Superior clutched the cross dangling from the heavy chain around her neck. How odd, she thought to herself, that she would seek protection in the one source she'd just affronted. "Your Excellency," she said, gripping the edge of her desk for support. "My apologies."

"What, no excuses?"

"Would you accept one?"

"I think you know the answer to that one," he purred, pivoting on his heel, so that he could avoid the direct sunlight.

Mother Superior noticed he didn't prefer the light. "Would you like me to draw the blinds?"

"No," he said stiffly, unwilling to offer much indulgence to any weakness. "You are finding my associates helpful?"

"Yes, Your Excellency, they've been very convincing and the plan is moving ahead smoothly."

"Not quite smoothly, is it Mother Superior?"

Her head bowed. "It is only a small difficulty, and can be -- will be -- easily dealt with."

"You choose your words carefully," he said, hands behind his back, cruising the length of the room, his pointed wings all but dragging the floor behind him.

She didn't even know his name. He liked it that way. If she'd wanted to tell anyone who he was, she'd be unable to. That was the way he wanted it. "I just wonder....."

"Then don't," he suggested, his words cold and merciless. "My time is running out, you see, Sister; and I'm afraid my plans will not wait for any impediments. But you knew this, of course, when you agreed to accept the terms of our arrangement."

Mother Superior squared her shoulders, trying to look confident.

"You have until tomorrow evening at six. By then you'll be enjoying your reward, or you'll be familiarizing yourself with the workings of local law enforcement." Then, he mumbled some words in a language she wasn't familiar with.

She was dumbstruck for a moment, clutching at her neck, her

mind muddled and confused. For a brief moment, the creature in front of her seemed less threatening; no more than a stranger you might pass in the hall. Just as she was taking a breath to speak, he was gone. She spun around the room, searching, but as usual, he left no trace. Mother Superior crumpled into her chair, racked with guilt and worry. How could she get this adoption through the system more quickly? This thing, this being, whatever it was, promised her the life she so desperately wanted.

Looking at the clock on the wall, she realized she didn't have the time to dwell on this particular problem. The Kingstons were coming for another visit with Wendy. The paperwork was progressing and by the end of the week, Wendy could be living with her new adoptive parents. She was doing a good thing, wasn't she?

Sarah Grace was the celebrity of the day. Never in her life had so many people touched her head in search of her all elusive bump. Just as she predicted, a simple trip to the pediatrician's office turned into a screaming ambulance ride to the emergency room where her brains were scooped off the floor and crammed back into her skull. Anyway, the extra attention was nice.

Wendy was acting as her personal assistant, and was pretty

good at shooing away the paparazzi, when she could see Sarah Grace was getting annoyed with the adulation. The girls went to sit under the only tree providing shade, and took out the chocolate chip cookies Velvet Littleton had tucked into her daughter's bag. Sarah Grace supposed her little bump rated an extra snack.

She stretched out under the tree and enjoyed her cookie. Father Francis had crossed her path several times that day, and each time she felt more in control. The only thing she couldn't figure out was if Father Francis was friend or foe. Fiona told her that changelings would work for anyone.

"Any more cookies?" Wendy asked.

"In my bag," she said, wiping the crumbs from her chin.

Wendy routed around in the bag, but instead of pulling out cookies, she pulled out Sarah Grace's blue pouch. "What's this?" she asked.

She sat up quickly, grabbed the pouch and stuffed it back into her book bag.

"What's wrong?" Wendy almost shouted. "I wasn't gonna hurt it."

"I know," Sarah Grace said, trying to regroup. "It's just, you know how it is with these nuns. They don't like to see lots of personal things from home." From Wendy's expression, she could see her friend wasn't exactly buying her explanation.

"What's in the bag, anyway?"

"Just a little bracelet my Momma gave me," she lied easily. "You know how it is. My brothers are always snooping in my room."

Wendy bowed her head. And Sarah Grace knew she'd touched a raw nerve. She didn't know how it was.

"I'm sorry," she said softly. "I didn't mean to be insensitive."

"I know," she said with a toss of her head. "But you know what? I may get to be an only child, and you know what that means?"

"Yeah," Sarah Grace smiled, "you'll get to shop 'til you drop, and your new parents will spoil you absolutely rotten."

"I'll have a blowout Sweet 16, they'll spend gobs of money, and I'll get a pink sports car," she added.

"But then, you'll be such a brat my parents won't allow me to be around you anymore," Sarah Grace laughed. She felt it. Her attention moved immediately past her friend to the people approaching with Mother Superior. The Kingstons!! They had to be changelings, too.

Wendy!!

"Hello, girls," Mother Superior greeted them.

Wendy stood up and brushed off her skirt. "Hi," she said cheerfully, moving toward the couple.

They seemed so sweet and normal, Sarah Grace thought. But she had no way of knowing whether they were good or bad. All she knew was that she couldn't let Wendy go away with them, until she could find out the truth.

Wendy pulled Mrs. Kingston closer to Sarah Grace. "This is my best friend in the whole wide world. Her name is Sarah Grace Littleton."

"Well, hello Sarah Grace," the couple greeted her in unison.

"Hi," she responded shyly. She didn't know how to read the couple. They seemed pleasant enough.

"Mr. and Mrs. Kingston," Mother Superior interrupted, "why don't you take Wendy to the library and you can visit for a while? She has a study hall next hour, so you'll have plenty of time."

"Can Sarah Grace come with us?" Wendy asked. "Sure, I'll come along," she said, grabbing her friend's hand.

"I'm afraid that wouldn't be the best idea," Mother Superior interrupted. There was a tension in her voice, which Sarah Grace had become very familiar with. It usually came out whenever they were within a mile of each other. "Wendy, you need to spend time alone with your prospective family."

"I know," Wendy said, "but Sarah Grace is my best friend. If you're going to be my family, you'd better get used to having her around," she giggled.

Sarah Grace watched the changelings carefully. She noticed they wouldn't take charge of the situation, that they made no plea on Wendy's behalf to indulge this request. They seemed to be little more than robots being manipulated by someone.

It was Mother Superior who had the last word. "Wendy, please? Why don't you take this meeting, and we'll see about including your friend the next time? Now hurry along. The Kingstons don't have all afternoon to visit."

Sarah Grace could see that Wendy was disappointed. "Go on Wendy," she coaxed. "You can tell me everything later." She smiled and nodded at the couple.

The three went off hand in hand, leaving Sarah Grace and Mother Superior under the tree. "They seem nice," she said, in as controlled a voice as possible.

To Mother Superior, the insinuation was all too plain. "I think Wendy will be very happy with them."

"They don't say much."

"Not everyone has to talk non-stop, Sarah Grace. You should try it some time," she suggested curtly, then turned and walked away.

But Sarah Grace didn't have time to deal with a cranky nun. She grabbed her book bag and took off toward the library. Making it there in record time, she stopped at the entrance and looked through the glass door. Wendy and the Kingstons were sitting at one of the low tables. From her appearance, she seemed happy. They were talking, smiling and laughing. If Sarah Grace didn't possess this unusual ability, she wouldn't have suspected a thing.

Another was near. Sarah Grace turned quickly to find Father Francis staring down at her.

"Shouldn't you be on your way to your next class?" he asked, looking at his watch. "The bell's already rung."

"I was just checking on Wendy. She's meeting with the Kingstons again, and she seemed a little nervous. Mother Superior said I couldn't go with her, so……"

"That's very kind of your Sarah Grace, but you shouldn't be late for class. I'm sure Wendy will be fine."

Sarah Grace watched his eyes and for the first time she noticed how lifeless they were. She thought he was trying to get her away from Wendy, which made her even more suspicious of his motives. But she was the child and he was the authority figure. The last thing she needed was another meeting with her parents. "Okay, Father."

They both reached for her book bag at the same time. Strangely, he was reluctant to release it, and his eyes drifted between Sarah Grace and the book bag. "Is something wrong?" she asked, gently tugging at the bag then throwing it over her shoulder.

"No," he said, shaking his head. "Your bag just seemed heavy. Are you sure you're not carrying too many books?"

"No, I'm fine," she assured him, taking off down the hall. She ducked into the girls' bathroom, leaned against the door and sighed. The pouch, she thought. He felt the weight of the pouch. Sarah Grace pulled the pouch from her bag and clipped it to the waistband of her shorts under her jumper. If Father Francis could feel the weight of the jewels in the pouch, the others would as well. "I should have left it at home," she scolded herself. It was safer being discovered by her snooping brothers.

"Sarah Grace?" Fiona called, appearing out of nowhere.

She almost jumped out of her skin, and her startled gasp echoed off the tile in the restroom. "I do wish you'd find a way to announce yourself without scaring the bejeezus out of me!"

"What are you doing in here?"

"Probably getting myself into even more trouble," she admitted, rubbing her face with her hand. "I'm supposed to be in class, but the Kingstons, I think they're changelings, like Father Francis."

"You mean the people who want to adopt Wendy?"

"Yes. They're in the library with her right now. I'm afraid to leave her, but if I don't get to class, I'll be in real trouble."

"Sarah Grace, you're already forgetting your training," Fiona fussed. "Ronan isn't the only one who can weave a time suspension spell!"

Her mouth fell open as her arms relaxed at her sides. She was so focused on her fear for her best friend she'd already forgotten that she had more than one way to shield her.

"You can do it, Sarah Grace," Fiona urged.

Taking that last bit of encouragement from her mentor, Sarah Grace took a cleansing breath and closed her eyes. She raised cupped hands to waist level. Fiona told her it was a way to center her power. Sarah Grace slowed her breathing, and before long, she felt the pouch of jewels warming at her side.

"Time and tide shall wait for me,

On land, the universe, the air, the sea,

Please hold them safely in your hand,

Until I release them, 'tis my command."

She felt a whoosh, as if water was rushing from ear to ear. Opening her eyes, she saw Fiona, fluttering happily in front of her.

"Go ahead," she urged, "open the door."

That trepidation was creeping in. She felt like Dorothy, opening the door of her little farmhouse once it had touched down in Oz. Except when she opened the door to the girls' restroom, she didn't see brilliant color and oversized flowers and mushrooms. There were the same drab beige halls she saw every day, except now the students and teachers were moving around her, but no one was acknowledging her existence.

She looked to her side and saw Fiona floating above her shoulder. "Did it work?"

"You bet your butt it did!!" the fairy exclaimed. "Sarah Grace, girl, you rock!"

Sarah Grace could only stare at the little creature. "You really need to stay away from the television." She stopped suddenly. Father Francis was less than three feet away.

"Don't worry," Fiona said, anticipating her fear. "If he's truly a changeling, he's also caught up in the spell. Only immortals are immune."

"That's good to know." They moved down the hall to the library. Wendy was still sitting there with the Kingstons. "Thank goodness."

"Sarah Grace, what exactly are you afraid of?" Fiona asked.

"That they'll take Wendy away before I can figure out how to save her. I don't trust Mother Superior. She throws them together every chance she gets, and Wendy's so in love with them, she can't talk about anyone else. If I tell her anything negative about these people, she won't believe me."

"True," she agreed, "but you're right. We've got to keep an eye on her."

"What do you mean, 'we'?" Ronan asked, as usual, appearing out of nowhere.

Sarah Grace wanted to offer him the same bit of advice she'd offered Fiona a few minutes ago, for all the good it would do her. They both popped in and out of her life, but he brought with him a certain abrasiveness. He wasn't necessarily unfriendly, but he wasn't always jovial.

"I can read your mind like a book, Fiona," he said.

"Well, if you already know what I want, why don't you stop grumbling and get to work?"

"Why you're welcome, Your Majesty," he said facetiously.

"You two fight more than my brothers," she observed. Sarah Grace watched the students and teachers in the classes drift through their work, completely unaware they were suspended in time. They would awaken from nothingness and continue on with their day as if nothing had ever happened. She'd done that.

Chapter 10

Sarah Grace couldn't relax until both she and Wendy were safely aboard the school bus at the end of the day. They usually held hands on the way to and from the bus, but today Sarah Grace seemed to need that lifeline more than ever. Her best friend was so happy. She thought all her dreams were about to come true, and had absolutely no comprehension about the conspiracy swirling around her. She chattered on relentlessly about the Kingstons, unaware they were little more than androids dressed up in a pleasing package. It took all of her composure not to expose them. But what would she say? Wendy was so wrapped up in her own world right now, she wasn't even interested in the fairy she'd met weeks ago.

The school year was coming to an end, and the relief was evident in every child. They were already discussing summer camps and vacation plans, and coming up with creative, not to mention destructive, ways of dispensing of any remaining school supplies. Uniforms would usually be first on the list, but they were too expensive to torch.

The bus hit a chuckhole in the dirt road that led out of town to the farming community. Every child was nearly tossed out of their seat, and enjoyed it thoroughly; but the bus was hot, and in these itchy uniforms, Sarah Grace sometimes found the ride uncomfortable. She wouldn't miss it.

"Hey," Wendy said, "if the Kingstons take me out, do you think your parents would let you go?"

"Oh, sure," she said, knowing very well the Kingstons would never invite her anywhere. "That'd be great."

They pulled up to Wendy's stop and Sarah Grace felt it. One of them was near, and it didn't take any magical power to figure out who or what it was. Wendy was waving good-bye, but Sarah Grace got up hastily and followed. "Wait, I'll go with you. My parents won't mind. We have to study for that English final anyway."

"Okay," Wendy beamed. She grabbed the girl's hand.

They were up the walkway and through the door in less than a minute. Wendy reacted with surprise when they entered the living room, but Sarah Grace's expression was steady. Mother Superior, Father Francis, the Kingstons, and Wendy's foster parents, Mr. and Mrs. Wilson, all rose to greet the girls. Sarah Grace saw at least one expression turn sour.

"Hi girls," said Mrs. Wilson, moving forward and putting an

arm around Wendy. "We've just been talking about your future, young lady," she smiled.

"Wendy," Mr. Wilson began, "This couple would like you to come and live with them."

"Oh, I know," she said cheerfully. "We've been visiting at school."

"Yes," said Mrs. Wilson.

"Wendy," Mother Superior spoke up. "The Kingstons have made up their minds."

Wendy looked hopefully at the couple, while Sarah Grace regarded the entire exercise with the cynicism it deserved. She watched Mr. Wilson and could see this was very hard for him. She'd always believed he wanted to keep Wendy. Sarah Grace's thoughts were interrupted by Wendy's cries of joy and the laughter of the adults in the room. Wendy was moving from person to person, hugging and thanking them. Eventually, Mother Superior's eyes rested on Sarah Grace, and while she said nothing, she was obviously feeling triumphant.

"If everything proceeds on schedule," said Father Francis, "Wendy could be in her new home by June 21st."

Sarah Grace's heart skipped a beat. Summer Solstice!!

"I know what you're thinking," Fiona said, almost out of breath. Sarah Grace was running, and the little fairy was having trouble keeping up; even in flight.

"Yeah, what am I thinking?" the girl asked in irritation.

"You're trying to figure out how to get Wendy out of there now; and if you get her out, what are you going to tell everyone when she disappears."

Sarah Grace stopped abruptly and Fiona smacked right into the side of her head. She bounced to the ground in a burst of golden dust, but Sarah Grace had not noticed. All her energy; all of her negative energy; was being focused on her guardian. She'd never felt such anger; such rage; such hatred. As the feeling began to overtake her, she felt heat pooling at her side. The pouch! Sarah Grace had forgotten all about it. Pulling up her jumper, she unclipped the pouch full of gemstones from her waistband, and held it away from her body. Taking several deep breaths, she forced herself to calm down, and as she did, the bag started to cool.

With a frown, she looked back at Fiona, who was sitting on an old log, readjusting her wings. "It was hot."

The fairy looked up. "What was hot?"

"My gem pouch. I was thinking about how much I hated Mother Superior and what she's trying to do, and the pouch got really hot. You didn't tell me that negative emotions could work like that."

Fiona cocked her head to the side. "Believe it or not, I was going to, and soon. I could see how you were beginning to feel. But don't give in to it, Sarah Grace. You open yourself up to your enemies in more ways than you know. It's a weakness, Sarah Grace, not a strength."

Lethargically, she let the pouch fall to her side. "Summer Solstice is two weeks away. I have fourteen days to put Wendy some place safe, and find out who Mother Superior is working for. More importantly, why my guardian, a nun, would turn from her vows to God, and to me."

"Weakness, Sarah Grace," Fiona muttered sadly. "There was something she wanted more than your safety, and someone knew that."

"But she's so openly hateful toward me. I don't understand it."

Fiona fluttered closer to her cailin. "But she doesn't

understand it either, Sarah Grace. Guardians don't just go bad. If a Droke is involved, her thoughts and actions have not been her own for some time. She could still be saved."

Sarah Grace shook her head. "No, I could never trust her again."

"Been there," Fiona said with wry amusement. "But you've got bigger fish to fry now."

"I know. I've got to put Wendy some place safe, find out who the real enemy is, and put an end to it all by Summer Solstice. Call Ronan back."

Fiona was stunned. It was the first time her cailin had given her an order. She watched this thin wisp of a girl raise her small hands and weave another time suspension spell around Wendy's home. But it wasn't her job to do this for Sarah Grace. She was a teacher and a guide. The spell was complete, so she looked at the girl and asked, "Now what?"

Sarah Grace was thoughtful for a moment. "Back to Mother Superior's office. It's time to find out who the enemy is."

Fiona was good for a great many things. When it came to moving from one spot to another, she was the best. Transport was instant, and in a heartbeat, they were back at the convent, inside Mother Superior's office.

"Why can't I do that?" Sarah Grace asked.

"I don't make up the rules," Fiona admitted. "Fairies get to pop in and out and use magic balls that look like flowers, and you get to battle villains. It's not a perfect world," she teased.

"Tell me about it." Sarah Grace didn't know how much time they had, so she quickly went through the drawers in the desk, deftly moving papers about and replacing them, to lessen the chance of suspicion. She closed the last drawer on a sigh. "Nothing." Sarah Grace looked under the desk, underneath the seat of the chair and in the closet. That's when she felt it again, except the sensation was so strong Sarah Grace felt as if her knees would buckle. Fiona swept her into the closet and closed the door.

"What is it?" the fairy asked, obviously concerned when she noticed the girl's stricken condition.

"I don't know," she whispered.

"Is it Mother Superior, Father Francis...."

"No, no," she gasped.

Startled, they both looked up when they heard a scraping

sound across the stone floor. It was slow and deliberate. There was a small circular grate on the closet door. Sarah Grace rose slowly on her tip toes and put her right eye next to Fiona who already had an excellent view. She'd gone oddly silent.

It was evil looking. The creature stood about eight feet tall, but the severely spiked wings, which jutted above its head made it seem like ten. Its body was human in form, but it wore something like an iridescent purple body suit. It didn't matter what it wore, Sarah Grace thought; it was ugly. The lower edges of its black wings were scraping the floor until it made a conscious effort to raise them. The thing finally turned toward them and Fiona gasped.

"Who or what is that thing?' Sarah Grace whispered.

"Branduff, the Black Raven," she whispered back.

"A Droke?"

"Yes."

"Why…?"

"Because his power is more potent. Compared to him, changelings are nothing. I had no idea that thing was involved."

Sarah Grace and Fiona felt like hostages in the small closet as

Branduff waited. And waited. Ten minutes passed and Sarah Grace could feel his agitation building. He was obviously waiting for Mother Superior, and she would not be here tonight; not until Sarah Grace released her.

Branduff went around to the other side of the desk and using one of his thickly pointed nails, scratched a message into the desk. Sarah Grace and Fiona covered their ears, as the sound was far worse than nails on a blackboard. With a final hiss, he was gone.

Sarah Grace began to feel better immediately, like she'd just gotten over a stomach flu. She opened the door and they went over to the desk to see what Branduff had written.

"A fortnight hence; like me, you will exchange this life for another."

"He didn't sign his name," Sarah Grace observed.

"He doesn't have to," Fiona reasoned. "She'll know exactly who left it. More's the pity." In all seriousness, she looked at her cailin. "Sarah Grace, you're going to have to help her now."

The girl's little brow wrinkled and she was filling up with righteous indignation. "I have to what?"

"You read the message. After he gets what he wants, he won't just release the woman. He'll take her back with him as a slave. I wouldn't wish that fate on my worst enemy."

"Just because she missed a meeting with him?"

"He never intended to release her, Sarah Grace. Branduff doesn't leave behind ties between this world and his."

So, she was being forced to help a person she viewed as an enemy. Could this situation get any weirder? "It's getting late. I'll have to release them," she muttered.

Mother Superior rushed into her office and slammed the door, out of breath, and frightened as she'd never been before. She couldn't understand how it had happened. She was never late for appointments and certainly not one as important as this. When she'd left Wendy's home, she checked her watch and realized she was more than thirty minutes behind schedule and panicked. Not that making the meeting would have been better for her. The most she could have hoped for was his mercy and an extension.

Mother Superior went over to her desk, but shock greeted her before she could even sit down. He'd been here already and the threat scrawled out on her desk was all the message she'd needed. She looked around the room, her paranoia increasing, hoping he wasn't lurking in the shadows. For the first time, she was beginning to wonder if she'd gone too far in her pursuit of what she believed she wanted.

Chapter 11

Fiona found Ronan and they returned to the big oak across the road. Now that the enemy had been revealed, Fiona wasted no time in alerting Queen Nivia and the Fae Counsel. Nivia's worst fears would be confirmed, and the worst possible scenario for Sarah Grace had presented itself. It was bad enough her guardian had betrayed her, but the culprit *behind* the plan would be more than enough for the little girl to deal with.

The Fae Counsel was brought together and the humor among the group was not good. The name of Branduff alone inspired every negative energy of such ferocity, it made it difficult for the Counsel to think and act as one.

"Silence," Queen Nivia commanded, raising her hand to the assemblage. "Silence, I say! Now that we know where the danger lies, we know where to strike."

"And strike with what?" one council member asked. "One newly trained cailin cannot protect us from Branduff."

"You don't know that!" Fiona countered. "My cailin is strong."

"But can she do it?" another asked.

"I cannot make you any promises," Fiona insisted, "just as you cannot make promises about the children you train. All I can tell you is that Sarah Grace has a compelling reason to focus her power and energy on ridding us all of Branduff. But she must move carefully. Once she strikes, her identity will be known, not only to Branduff, but to others."

"Regardless," Ronan pressed, "we need not waste time here, wondering what she can or cannot do. Fiona and I need to get back."

Fiona was thankful. Ronan always cut right to the heart of the matter, and she was tired of this inquisition.

Queen Nivia agreed and sent them on their way. The council had their work to do as well. Should Sarah Grace fail, the Queen would need to use every other weapon in her arsenal to keep the Tree of Promise safe and out of Branduff's reach.

"Your Highness," one of the council asked, "why should we trust an inexperienced cailin to take care of one as treacherous as Branduff? Should you not intervene now?"

"We cannot be the first line of defense to save the human world," Nivia reasoned. "This is not the only threat they will face, and if they do not learn now how to protect themselves, how long do you think they will last in this universe?"

"I find no comfort in your assessment," another fairy said.

"Your comfort is not my present concern," the Queen told them sternly. "This is how it has always been and always will be. Who are we to break the ancient chain?"

The group grumbled momentarily, then silenced itself.

"Now go, all of you," Nivia commanded, tired of their whining. "You all have preparations to make."

Thousands of yellow points of light dispersed among the various natural outgrowths, leaves and crevices of bark in the tree. Each fairy had a portal to protect and immediately set to weaving spells of protection to make those portals stronger against any intruder. Nivia sent word through a Grogoch to seal the entrance to the Tree of Promise, as well as doubling the guard.

A golden basin was brought to her. It was filled with water scented with nectar. Nivia washed her hands and face, then dried them a delicate rose petal. She looked about herself. The tree was alive with activity. And fear.

Sarah Grace was feeling somewhat triumphant. The enemy --

all the enemies she thought had been identified -- and now, all that was left was the plan for their destruction. Once they were gone, not only was her world safe, but so was her best friend. She felt like she could fly as she raced down the walkway to the front door of her home. Reaching for the door knob, she almost fell forward as the door was jerked open from the other side.

"Where have you been, Sarah Grace?" her father asked.

His expression was grim and he seemed very tense. "I was just exploring in the woods and forgot about the time," she said, walking inside. Sarah Grace was getting very good at telling little white lies to cover her absences. It was always convenient to suspend time to keep her family from suspecting.

But as she moved further into the living room, she could feel the intense mood. Her brothers were standing beside Momma, who was seated in a recliner by the window. Momma was crying softly to herself.

"What's wrong, Momma?" she asked, looking around the room at all the distressed faces. Then she noticed something. "Where's Grammy?"

Velvet Littleton only cried harder. Jonathan moved closer and put his arm around his mother.

Sarah Grace felt her father's meaty arm descend upon her shoulders. Instinctively, she shrank from his hold. "Where's Grammy?" she asked with more urgency.

"Sarah Grace," he said, taking her by the shoulders, "she's gone."

"Where?" she cried, shaking her head, because she knew what he meant.

"Sarah Grace…"

She was already down the hall, pushing open the door of her grandmother's room. It was empty.

Fiona and Ronan didn't understand it. Fairies were told when one life force ended, another would begin. That's why they didn't understand it. As they looked upon the funeral rites of Sarah Grace's grandmother, what was the sadness about? Why were they crying? Why hadn't Sarah Grace spoken to them in the last three days leading up to the funeral? Why were they all dressed in black?

"It's quite curious," Ronan said, his head cocked to one side. "Death is a part of their human life. Why should they carry on so?"

Fiona had no real answers for him. She suspected it was how she felt when Orva betrayed her. She suspected. Somehow, Fiona thought Sarah Grace's hurt went a lot deeper than that.

The mourners were moving away from the gravesite to their cars. Fiona watched as Sarah Grace, clinging to her mother, got into the family's car, her head still bowed.

Fiona had tried not to intrude, since her first contact with her cailin after her grandmother's death. The grief was too fresh and the young girl had shut down every emotion, in order to deal with her loss. Fiona had spent the last three nights, hovering over her bed, weaving spells to help her sleep, anything that would give her some relief. But she always found the relief to be short in duration. The minute Sarah Grace's eyes opened, that fleeting moment of normalcy instantly disappeared, and she was once again remembering why she had been so weary the night before.

The mourners were at her home now, eating. Another strange custom Fiona didn't understand. She didn't see Sarah Grace, even though Wendy was among the mourners. Fiona went to her room, which was empty. She continued to move through the other rooms of the house, and found Sarah Grace in the last one - - Grammy's.

She was sitting at the vanity, mindlessly going through the many ornate boxes with their loose gemstones, tangled necklaces and bracelets. Sarah Grace always knew these things would one day belong to her. She hadn't suspected that day would come so soon. She put her head down on her arms and sighed.

Fiona moved closer and took a seat on one of the jewelry boxes. She didn't know what to say, but she hoped that her presence would be of some comfort to the little girl.

Sarah Grace couldn't wait for all those people to leave. She couldn't take one more person hugging or kissing her, telling her everything would be all right. It wouldn't be. Things wouldn't be all right for a very long time.

She lay in Grammy's bed, wrapped up in one of the old quilts she'd made quite some time ago, willing herself into a dreamless sleep, that was slow in coming. The sun had gone down a couple of hours ago, and thankfully, her family had let her go off on her own.

If she closed her eyes, the scents of the bedroom crept into her mind. The old fabric of the quilt she lay under, the perfumes Grammy dabbed on her inner wrists, the oil she put in her hair, all those things created a person whose arms were around her.

Around her?

Sarah Grace sat up, but the embrace continued. She drew back, and only then did she notice the light. There were arms around her, she could feel it. She could see the light.

Suddenly, the embrace was broken, and Sarah Grace felt alone again, except for….there was something large and lumpy under her hip. She moved off the object and turned on the bedside light. "My gem pouch," Sarah Grace said out loud; but no. This was not her pouch. It was green, not blue, and the material was worn, almost thread-bare. The initial 'M' had been embroidered into the material, but a good deal of the thread was now gone.

Sarah Grace looked back at Grammy's vanity. The jewels. All those loose gemstones. "Fiona!" she called in a vigorous whisper. "Fiona, I know you're there. Reveal yourself!"

"You don't have to shout at me," Fiona admonished. I just wanted to give you some time. What's wrong?"

"What is this?" the girl asked, holding up the pouch.

"I don't know. It's not mine and it's not yours," she answered, her brow drawn together in a frown. "Who's 'M'?"

Sarah Grace looked at the bag again. "Madeline. My Grammy's first name was Madeline. That's what she was trying to tell me," she said jumping from the bed and running over to the vanity. She dumped the jewelry boxes out and stones fell recklessly over the glass surface.

Fiona buzzed over her shoulder, speechless for one of the first times in her life. Sarah Grace's grandmother had been a 'cailin'.

"She was trying to tell me," Sarah Grace told Fiona, the tears she'd been holding off finally flowing freely. "I couldn't believe it, but now I know she was trying to tell me she was a cailin."

"I'm sorry, Sarah Grace," Fiona said sympathetically. "I had no idea."

"She could see that I was scared and nervous about things. And she understood. Why couldn't I see it? I have so many questions that only another cailin could answer for me. Why didn't I see it?" She hugged the bag to her chest. Fiona fluttered closer and stroked the child's hair. "She knew how special you were, just like me. She was strong and I know she'd want you to be the same way."

Sarah Grace sniffled and dragged a fist under her nose. "I felt her, Fiona. I felt her hugging me. Am I crazy?"

"I don't think so. If you say you felt her, I believe you. Sarah Grace, don't you believe, in your religion, I mean, that you'll see your loved ones again? In Heaven?"

Sarah Grace nodded shakily.

"Well, if you will, why are you so sad?"

"I guess because it seems so far away. I can't see her again until I die. And like my mother says, God willing, that won't be for a long time."

"But you've got her pouch and her hugs until then, don't you?"

She looked at the gem pouch and remembered the feeling of the embrace. "All right, Fiona. Back to work."

She was moving so quickly the air caught her habit and she looked almost like a raven in flight. Mother Superior rounded the corner of the building adjacent to the playground in great haste. She'd waited patiently on the landing above the courtyard, watching the children get off the bus in the morning. Wendy had not gotten off the bus. But Sarah Grace had.

The woman stopped in her tracks as she spied the impish fifth grader leaning against a tree, watching her. Her book bag was slung across her shoulder, and but her head was bent slightly to the side, almost as if she were listening to someone speak in whispers. Sarah Grace's lips never moved, but she did nod once or twice. Never did she take her eyes off Mother Superior as she moved forward.

Sarah Grace straightened as the nun got closer.

"Good morning, Sarah Grace," she said, fixing a strained smile to her lips. "I was so sorry to hear about your grandmother."

"Thank you."

"Can you tell me where Wendy is?"

"No," the girl said simply.

Mother Superior stiffened. "But you're best friends. Is she ill?"

"No."

Her responses were almost robotic, completely devoid of emotion. Mother Superior's anxiety was rising. She was close to shaking the information out of the girl. "Perhaps I should call her foster parents?"

Sarah Grace only nodded, picked up her bag and headed off to class.

Mother Superior's fists were balled at her sides, her nails digging into her palm. Any longer and she'd draw her own blood. She rushed back to her office to make that phone call.

"She's cracking," Fiona said to Sarah Grace.

"I know," Sarah Grace told her. "She'll never get Wendy, though," she said with some satisfaction.

"Sarah Grace!"

She groaned. It was Devon. Fiona disappeared as she turned to face her classmate.

"Hey," he said quietly.

"Hi."

"You okay?" he said, his eyes dropping to his feet.

She nodded. She'd guessed all the kids in the school had heard about her grandmother.

"Look, I was wondering….sometimes I like to hike around the woods."

"Yeah."

"You wanna go sometime?"

"Why?" she wondered aloud. Devon had never asked her to do a thing in her life.

"I just thought it would be fun. Besides," he laughed, "it's a bigger place to chase me." He nudged her shoulder as he sauntered off down the hall.

Sarah Grace shook her head as she watched him go.

The phone at the Wilson's home rang relentlessly. No answering machine or cell phones. The Wilsons were plain people. A simple home, their needs met financially, probably a little nest egg, and enough to take a little vacation in the summer, were all they seemed to require. They seemed happy, like most of the people living in the surrounding farm community. How could they be happy with so little? Of course, they could be happier. They had no children of their own.

Something else was nagging at her. Replacing the receiver on its cradle, she let her hand fall to the desk and took a deep breath. Mother Superior knew that the Wilsons wanted Wendy. Mrs. Wilson had told her on more than one occasion that if Associated Catholic Charities had not been able to find Wendy a permanent home, she and her husband would be glad to have her. But she'd told the woman they'd been looking for a younger couple, not one in their early fifties. Of course, that had been a cruel lie. There was no such regulation. Wendy was almost a teenager, not an infant. Parents having their first child in their thirties and forties was now the norm, not the exception.

She jumped up and went to the window. Looking across the compound, she saw a shadow passing behind the stained glass windows on the opposite building. The chill rushing up her spine was all the reminder she needed. Mother Superior stepped back from the window, ran to the door and jerked it open. "Oh!"

"Mother Superior, is everything all right?" She was met with the anxious expression of Sister Beatrice.

"No, no," she said, catching her breath and gathering her wits. "I was expecting another appointment."

"Then, I won't keep you," the nun said obligingly. "I just wanted to leave these vaccination records for Wendy in your office. They'll be needed for the adoption. How is that going, by the way?"

The woman nodded nervously. "Just fine, just fine. Thank you, Sister," she said, taking the documents. After the nun left, Mother Superior tossed the papers on her desk, then hurried to the car used by the parish. She had to get to Wendy's home and find out what was going on. If the adoption fell through, everything she had worked for would crash and burn around her.

As the steel grey sedan pulled out of the parking lot, Mother Superior had the feeling she was being watched. She was absolutely right.

Approaching the Wilson's home, Mother Superior could see Wendy passing by the picture window in the front room. She was dressed in her school uniform, with a tray full of snacks in her hands. As Mother Superior got closer, she also saw the Wilsons sitting on the sofa in front of the television. Wendy sat down and put the tray on her foster mother's lap.

Mother Superior knocked. She knocked again and again. The Wilsons would not answer. She went back to the window and saw them still in front of the television. "Hello!!" she called, then knocked on the window. "Mr. and Mrs. Wilson, hello!" They wouldn't answer. What's going on? She tried to open the front door, but it was locked and she certainly didn't want to risk trying to force her way into the home. Her anxiety level increased as she returned to the car and drove back to school.

She felt defeated and afraid, as she went back to her office later in the day. She hadn't returned right away, fearful of facing him, but realizing that if he wanted to find her, he would. Mother Superior felt as if she were drowning in her own deceit. How much had she risked for something which might be ultimately unattainable?

Letting herself into her office and closing the door, she leaned against it and closed her eyes. Something caught her eye. Something was sparkling on her desk, something that hadn't been there when she left. Mother Superior approached the desk slowly. It was a diamond, a large one! She grabbed it! Was it genuine?

"Oh, it's real."

The small but firm voice came from across the room. Mother Superior knew who it was. "How did you get into my office?"

Sarah Grace walked out from a dark corner, her pouch of jewels tied at her side. Fiona and Ronan fluttered behind her, still unseen to the nun. "If I told you, you wouldn't believe me," the girl said dryly.

"If you leave at once, I won't call your parents," she said sternly, closing her fist around the diamond.

"I think it's about four carats. You can probably get a lot of money for it."

"What are you talking about?" the woman snapped.

"My diamond. I left it on the desk."

"Where would you get a stone like this?" Mother Superior demanded. "Did you steal it?"

"That's good, coming from you," Sarah Grace teased, sarcastically. "Money's become very important to you, hasn't it Mother Superior? So important you were willing to sell my friend."

"What do you mean?" she demanded, insulted she was being interrogated by a student.

"This adoption," Sarah Grace reminded her. "It came up out of nowhere, didn't it?"

"That's none of your…"

"And why Wendy?" she continued. "This school is full of children in foster care. Why my best friend?"

Fiona and Ronan watched the exchange and began to think Sarah Grace was straying from her intended mission. Her anger was rising and that's not what they needed. They fluttered closer.

"What's so special about your friendship?" Mother Superior sneered. "One brat is pretty much like another. But you're right.

I'd be less than honest if I told you I didn't take a special delight in removing Wendy from your life."

She was about to ask why, when the feeling hit her again. Sarah Grace backed away. The crystals at her side were warming again, and she realized she'd forgotten what Fiona had told her.

"Leave my office," Mother Superior demanded, flinging her arm toward the door, her face contorted with anger. "You've interfered in my affairs for the last time," she shouted, the threat in her voice imminent.

But Sarah Grace hadn't heard her. The feeling was getting stronger, twisting like an iron vice around her heart. It was Branduff.

"Sarah Grace," Fiona called, tugging at one of her braids.

"He's coming," Ronan warned, fluttering off a spot above the closet.

Sarah Grace could not get past her anger, and before she could regain her focus, the room filled with a hazy purple light that quickly dissipated. Branduff appeared, the smile on his face emitting not one bit of compassion.

Fiona disappeared inside the collar of Sarah Grace's shirt and pinched her hard. She wasn't allowed to help her cailin, other than offering advice and direction. No matter how hard it was for Sarah Grace, Fiona could only sit back and watch.

Branduff was vile, just as she'd remembered. Sarah Grace had been repulsed by his appearance before, but now, face to face with his evil, she could see why the Fae world was in danger. He paid virtually no attention to Mother Superior, except to open his hand -- actually it was more like a claw -- in her direction. Without a word, she dropped the diamond into his palm. Her demeanor had changed. Clearly, she had disappeared into her subconscious and was no longer aware of what was unfolding around her.

"It's really quite useless to question her motives," he said, his voice smooth, the tone deep and mesmerizing. "She can't remember what her true 'calling' is." Then he laughed, a sound so malevolent it made the hair on the back of her neck stand up. Mother Superior had long ago shrank under his gaze and was content to stand at his side like an obedient pet.

"Her mind hasn't been her own since she entered into this deal. She's a foolish woman; one who's let her need for recognition and power bring her to this," he said, transferring the diamond slowly from one palm to the other. "Unfortunately, Mother Superior has confused the two. Power isn't about the material things one can possess. Don't you agree, cailin?"

Sarah Grace's expression remained unchanged.

"Yes, I know what you are," he admitted, his lips curling into a callous, ruthless smile. "I also know this isn't the only jewel you possess."

"Why do you need the jewels?"

"Ah, it speaks! These pretty rocks are payment for the changelings. They can be rather crude; what your kind might refer to as 'trailer trash'. They like jewels, currency, anything they can exchange for whatever it is a changeling would want."

Sarah Grace took a step forward, perhaps trying to show him that she wasn't totally afraid of him. "How much did you offer them to act as Wendy's adoptive parents?"

"Virtually nothing," he mused, standing up. "The bulk of the payment will go for capturing your friend and bringing her to me."

She smiled. She knew Wendy and her foster parents were still under the influence of the time suspension spell.

"Oh, such confidence," he teased, moving past Mother Superior and rounding the desk, coming to stand just three feet away from her. "There's only one thing I need from your friend. Once I have that, you may have her, all of her back. After all, I'll have no need of the lifeless body left, once I've taken the essence."

Sarah Grace jumped back and put her hand to her side, touching the pouch.

His gaze traveled downward to the little blue pouch and he smiled again. "Well, you've mastered many lessons, I see," he said, obviously estimating the number of stones in the bag. "I can tell you'll be a worthy adversary."

Chapter 12

He flicked a hand at Mother Superior, rendering her as still as a statue, but as he turned toward Sarah Grace, her small hand went up as well and put a box of frozen glass around Branduff. Drokes hated the cold, and although he could certainly get out, it would give Sarah Grace a couple of precious minutes to escape. She grabbed her gem pouch and ran past Mother Superior, who would be quite safe as she was. Fiona and Ronan were at her shoulders.

They heard Branduff scratching and clawing at the frozen glass, knowing every time he touched it, he'd be subjected to a burn, and every time he did that he'd get angrier. Sarah Grace threw open a window at the end of the hall and reached into her pouch. She took an emerald and tossed it out onto the ground. Putting her hand out, she simply said, "Grow." Within seconds, a strong leafy stalk was at her disposal.

As she climbed out on the ledge, she felt a shudder that made her think the building was about to collapse. Branduff came crashing through the wall of Mother Superior's office, angry, with bluish abrasions covering his body. His chest was heaving, and Sarah Grace could see the unvarnished anger in his eyes. She jumped out onto the stalk and said, "Shrink." Branduff appeared at the window as the stalk sank and deposited Sarah Grace safely to the ground. She took off across the grass, her small companions behind her.

Branduff jumped from the window and hit the ground in hot pursuit, wincing each time his bruises came in contact with the leaves of bushes and low hanging branches from trees.

Sarah Grace made it to the parking lot, and once again raised her hand to leave a sheet of ice behind her, but Branduff had apparently decided he could no longer take her inexperience for granted. He shrank himself to Fiona's size and jumped onto a plastic lid which had been discarded by one of the students. Sarah Grace, Fiona and Ronan, disappeared into the wooded area just beyond the school grounds and ducked into a grove of trees. A leafy canopy rose high above them, blocking out the light.

Sarah Grace took several red and yellow stones from her pouch and scattered them in a staggered fashion across the space around them. They all looked up suddenly. They could hear him. Branduff was huffing in pain, but getting closer as the sound of breaking bushes and twigs got louder.

"Hurry!" Fiona insisted.

Completing her task, Sarah Grace picked up the pouch and Fiona and Ronan followed her to a small stream, which they crossed on the rocks. Looking back, she smiled. Every time Branduff stepped on a stone, a burst of flame erupted at his feet.

His screams kept them on the run. So far she'd been lucky.

Nivia agreed, watching the three move on to their next target. An anxious crowd of fairies surrounded the Queen, gazing into her flower ball, holding their collective breaths, indulging a hope, this cailin would be successful. This was as near to the Tree of Promise as they'd ever wanted something like Branduff to be.

Now, Sarah Grace was huffing and puffing. She'd been running for the last twenty minutes without rest, with the anxiety of a monster chasing her adding to the apprehension. She ducked behind a large grouping of rocks.

"Sarah Grace, you can't stop now," Ronan told her, tugging on a pigtail. "That thing is close on our heels."

"Ronan's right," Fiona insisted. "We've got to get him into the open. The moon is rising."

"I know," Sarah Grace hissed. "I know." She bent down and put her hands on her knees. She was tired and scared and angry.

She could feel the pouch warming at her side as her gaze traveled upward. They took off again. They had to get back to the tree farm.

Branduff was in greater pain. In his anger and distress, he'd let his pride get the better of him. An untried cailin had him screaming and oozing his own fluid. Though no blood circulated through his vein, no breathing creature was made of dust alone. A grey sludge wept from cuts and abrasions, and with every drop spilt, his substantial strength was being diminished. He slowed down to consider his predicament. Getting past the last of the stones the girl had tossed to the ground, he was all but safe for now. Looking at the many wounds on his once sleek body made him tense once more. Think! Think!, he willed himself. He needed to get at that other girl. She was an easier target than the cailin herself. Nivia had to be watching her. That she had such powers meant her Fae counsel was with her. Why had he wasted so much time with that foolish, greedy nun?

Branduff looked upward. As the evening wore on, the elements would become his constant enemy as well. Before the moon was over the trees, Sarah Grace Littleton would be sorry she'd ever been contacted by the Fae.

"I've never walked all the way home," Sarah Grace said, sure she was going to expire at any time. They weren't quite at her home, though. The trio stopped across the road about one hundred yards from the Tree of Promise. Branduff had to be near the tree when the moon was just above the trees. They had to be near Nivia, just in case.

"It's too quiet," Ronan grumbled. "I don't like it when it's this quiet." He looked over his shoulder; then down the road. Satisfied he had a second or two, the Grogoch buzzed into a dirt mound and rooted around in it for a moment or two. Backing out of it, he sneezed and brown dust went everywhere.

"What are you doing?" Fiona insisted, flitting over to him.

Ronan shook off his dirt-encrusted hand, then opened it so Fiona could see.

Her eyes were wide with amazement, and a slow indulgent smile framed her face. "Where did you get that?" she asked, gazing at a large black diamond in that grubby hand.

"Dig long enough and you never know what you'll find."

"Yuck," Sarah Grace said, comparing the dark jewel to the more colorful ones in her pouch. "Who'd want that thing?"

"Fiona?"

"I know," the fairy said, "I didn't get around to every lesson."

"This is a fine time to tell her," Ronan said gruffly, looking over his shoulder. It had been quiet for too long.

"What does it mean, Fiona?"

Fiona never got a chance to answer. All of a sudden a low rumbling began to fill their ears. Branduff was chanting in some kind of long forgotten language Fiona had never heard before. The three were almost frozen with fear, and they could feel the vibrations of trees falling, and stones being tossed out of the way. Sarah Grace fumbled in the bag for a green stone. She threw it toward the sound, and a thick stalk sprang up from the ground, just as Branduff appeared. The tip of the stalk caught him on the nose and he howled in pain. Sarah Grace ran from the clearing, but Branduff's chanting continued. She felt herself getting weaker, and her feet just wouldn't do what she wanted them to.

"Come on, Sarah Grace," Fiona cried, tugging at the girl's collar.

Ronan tried to offer some assistance, but suddenly felt himself flying against a tree under someone else's power. Branduff snorted, and the force of it sent Fiona into the canopy.

Sarah Grace looked up, tired, breathing deeply, her heart wrapped with a fear she'd never known. She couldn't see Fiona or Ronan and at this moment, she'd never felt so alone or unprepared in her entire life.

His chest was heaving, his red eyes were brilliant with renewed anger, and his mouth curled into a malevolent smile. Effortlessly, his huge clawed hand snatched up her pouch.

Sarah Grace was feeling even weaker. Her head was spinning and she felt sick to her stomach. It was the same feeling she'd had before she learned to control her emotions, upon the sighting of someone from the Fae world. Then she remembered what Fiona had told her. If she ever lost possession of her gems, she'd be vulnerable, that her power would not be as strong.

"What is it, Sarah Grace?" he teased. "Not feeling like yourself?" His laugh was meant to chill the blood in her veins, and it almost did. "I'm afraid I'm suffering from the same affliction," he said, gesturing to the many wounds on his purple body. "Not to worry, cailin. They'll heal much more quickly than yours will," he said, pulling a red stone from the bag and tossing it just inches from her head. The bush behind her lit up like flaming star bent on destruction.

With all her might she rolled away to a safer distance. Where were Fiona and Ronan?

Branduff knelt down and eyed her with a facetious fear. A hand neared her face and she backed away.

"You're right to be afraid," he said, his voice more menacing. "If you'd had more respect for my power, you might not have played all these nasty little tricks on me."

"But you're so much fun to hurt," she said, hoping the waver in her voice was barely detectable.

"Ah, our little cailin has a spine after all," he said with a wink. He playfully tossed her gem pouch into the air and caught it in his hand. "Thank you for the gift, little cailin. And now, I have one for you." He motioned to his left.

Sarah Grace's heart crumbled. "Wendy!"

The changelings certainly looked different. Gone was the façade of two middle class parents with sweet smiles and affectionate looks. They were now the grubbiest of fairies with deadpan faces, fluttering above her best friend's head.

"Wendy," she called, getting up; the sheer concern for the

girl's well-being propelling her forward. She moved closer, but just as she got a foot away, she bounced back as a brilliant gold light flashed.

"I believe the changelings call it a cloaking field," Branduff explained. "Not to worry, though. Wendy is unaware of what's happening around her."

"What have you done with the Wilsons?"

"Who?"

"Her foster parents, butthead!"

Branduff frowned. "Butthead? What does that mean?"

"Just what you think it does." Sarah Grace calmed herself. Fiona told her that letting her anger get the best of her diluted her strength, and she needed every ounce of that strength to get them out of this mess.

Fiona sat up and shook her head. That snort of Branduff's sent her flying into hard contact with a tree branch. Oddly, it reminded her of her first meeting with Sarah Grace. Blinking her eyes, she looked around and was unfamiliar with her surroundings. "Sarah Grace? Ronan?"

"Fiona," Ronan called, crawling over the ground cover at the base of the trees. "Where have you been? I've looked all over for you."

"I've been right here, unconscious. Oh my gosh, where's Sarah Grace?"

"In trouble."

"I've just figured out what 'butthead' means," Branduff snorted, "and I'm sure it's not complimentary."

"So you're a butthead and a little dim-witted as well?" Sarah Grace taunted.

"Perhaps in your estimation," he answered grimly. "I have full control of my power. It's unfortunate you cannot say the same. The minute you were distracted, your spell began to weaken, making it simple to get to my prey," he smiled, gesturing to Wendy.

Sarah Grace would not make that mistake again. She had to lure him into the open and she had very little time to do it. She looked at her friend. The changelings above her had been silent and were pretty much as they'd been described. Mercenaries for hire. Her pouch was still pretty heavy, but it was in his hand, not hers.

Wendy was safe as she was right now, she thought to herself, as she slowly began to back out of the glen. Branduff's eyes narrowed, but when she broke out into a run, he roared his discontent. Sarah Grace felt the ground shaking beneath her feet for every step he took, as she ducked from tree to tree, trying to throw him off. She reached a small earthen ledge and jumped down into a shallow hole, which revealed a tiny cave. Scrambling in, she watched as he stormed past her.

Once she was sure he was a safe distance away, Sarah Grace ran back to the clearing. The changelings were still standing by dutifully with Wendy in a serene trance. They weren't the only ones in the clearing. She saw Fiona and Ronan fluttering into view.

"Where have you been?" she asked, exasperated and relieved at the same time.

"Sorry," Fiona apologized, "but he almost put me out of commission with that snort of his."

"Where is he now?" Ronan asked.

"Chasing a ghost," Sarah Grace, grimaced. "Look, I've got to get Wendy out of here. I was just about to weave a time suspension spell around the changelings."

"I've got a better idea," Ronan said, putting that black diamond in her hand.

"What am I supposed to do with this thing?" Sarah Grace asked, sure that Branduff would be on his way at any time.

"It's as valuable as everything in your pouch," Ronan snapped at her. "Need I remind you that yours is missing!"

"I couldn't help it!" she snapped back, snatching the gem and moving closer to the changelings. Sarah Grace held out her hand, and said, "For her release."

One of the changelings was clearly impressed, but the other showed little emotion. Still, it held out its hand and accepted the gem. It turned it in its palm and inspected it thoroughly, taking special note of the color and its weight. The changeling looked at the hopeful group, then nodded at his companion. The duo floated back and their bonds on Wendy dissolved. Without a word, they disappeared.

Wendy was disoriented, but they had no time to explain to her what had happened. They could hear Branduff returning. Sarah Grace grabbed her friend's hand and pulled her along. They had only minutes to lure Branduff into the clearing.

Branduff pounded the ground with his fists. She'd gotten

away from him again, the little imp. The changelings were gone and so was the child. He needed her to achieve immortality, and he didn't have the time to snatch another child. That tree!! That damned tree!! Nivia sat in ultimate power over him and his only chance of changing the dynamic, was slipping through his fingers.

He knew where they'd gone. His only option was to follow.

Sarah Grace hid Wendy near a grouping of shrubs, with promises of an explanation as soon as her head cleared. She had to get to work. "Ronan, could you stay near her?"

"Yes," the Grogoch said, sounding almost proud he had been given the responsibility.

Sarah Grace did a double take. It was the first time Ronan had ever spoken to her without his trademark sarcasm. He settled next to Wendy.

"Come on," she beckoned Fiona. They moved to the most open part of the field, where there was a collection of four stones. Sarah Grace pulled a piece of charcoal from her pocket and knelt down in front of the first stone. She took a moment to collect herself.

"Hurry, Sarah Grace," Fiona urged.

She had to draw symbols on four stones, a binding spell that would destroy Branduff. The symbols were a combination of geometric figures. Now she wished she'd paid more attention in math class. The first was a circle with a triangle inside. The second, a square with a five pointed star. The third, a triangle with a diamond. And the fourth......

The brutal vibration of Branduff landing just yards from her made Sarah Grace drop the charcoal and she landed on her bottom. Fiona darted behind her.

Branduff shook a chastising finger at her. "No drawing, Sarah Grace," he teased, moving closer. He tossed the bag of jewels into the air and caught them. "If you can't finish your pretty masterpiece, it won't matter where I'm standing or when, will it?"

Sarah Grace was scrambling for the charcoal, but every time she moved, Branduff put a foot down in front of her.

Ronan was watching from their hiding place. Wendy was still a little fuzzy. She was lying down, somewhere between sleep and consciousness. Ronan buzzed toward the clearing, pulling a piece of jagged metal from his pocket. With Branduff concentrating on taunting Sarah Grace, he raced to Branduff's face, dragging the piece of metal across his eye.

The ensuing scream shook the trees as the Droke raised his hands to the injury and dropped the pouch of gems. Branduff stumbled, blinded, and Sarah Grace grabbed the charcoal. Quickly, she drew the last symbol on the stone, picked up her pouch, and with the fairies at her shoulders, dashed over to the bushes where Wendy lay.

There was a piercing silence around them. The wind stopped, the birds in the area moved on, and the crickets stopped chirping. Branduff's moans had ceased, and now it was just him and his anger, once more. His gaze was drawn upward as a brilliant light appeared over his head. A large star was visible and shards of light shot out from its center.

"No!" Branduff cried. "No!"

Sarah Grace, Fiona and Ronan covered their ears as his cries increased, but they couldn't take their eyes off what was happening. Sarah Grace had never seen anything like it before. Those shards of light shot through Branduff's body and out of each of his wounds until one couldn't tell where the star began and the creature ended. Sarah Grace stood slowly as it began to morph from something evil to something beautiful.

He was gone.

All that was left was the star. The star spun toward the heavens, then stopped in the place where it began, cool and serene.

Sarah Grace moved to the spot just underneath that star. Ronan and Fiona joined her, with Wendy falling in behind.

"What in the world happened?" the girl asked. "Sarah Grace? How did I get here?" she wondered, pulling little bits of grass from her hair.

Fiona buzzed to her side. "Well done, cailin," she said.

"Well done," Ronan repeated.

Sarah Grace looked at him for a moment. "Thank you, Ronan. If it hadn't been for you…"

"All I did was distract him," he insisted.

"We weren't supposed to help her," Fiona said.

"You weren't supposed to help her," he reminded her. "Nothing in the rules said I couldn't help."

Back at the school, Mother Superior was jolted by an unknown force. She gripped the side of her desk to steady herself. Trying to clear her head, a sudden realization swept over her. "Oh my God," she whispered, placing trembling fingers on her forehead. It all came rushing back to her. "What have I done?"

"You betrayed your child," came a voice from the dark interior of the room.

Mother Superior turned toward the voice and was met with the ethereal light of Queen Nivia. She immediately bowed her head. "Your Highness," she gasped, 'please…"

Nivia moved forward. "Your apologies are not necessary," she said. "It is not an uncommon occurrence for a guardian to be compromised by an enemy. Regardless, your tenure here has come to an end."

Mother Superior said nothing, but simply nodded.

"You will be reassigned in some other capacity."

She nodded again. There was nothing left to say, no need to defend her actions. No petty pleas would make any difference. She had failed and would not be trusted with the welfare of any child, ever again.

Nivia took Mother Superior with her. Her fate would not be

known for some time, but Mother Superior welcomed the time to reflect. She was sure of one thing. She'd rather go with Nivia in disgrace than be a slave at Branduff's will.

Epilogue

"Bye Momma, bye Daddy!" Wendy called to her parents as she ran down the walkway to meet Sarah Grace at the gate. The adoption papers had been signed two months ago and now Wendy had a forever home. With Sarah Grace and her brothers down the road, it was like having a sister and two brothers. They seemed to tease her just as much as their own sister.

"Come on, Wendy," Sarah Grace said, grabbing her hand. "They're waiting for us."

Things were certainly looking up. Through the grapevine, the girls heard that Mother Superior and Father Francis had left the school for 'undisclosed' reasons. The tongue wagging across the backyard fences was pretty intense for a few weeks and many theories were floated as to why they actually departed, but Sarah Grace just looked on the whole affair with a certain calm. She knew why they were gone, and the reasons were far worse than a few dollars missing from the church coffers.

Today was about celebration and friendship. Sarah Grace couldn't share everything about what she was with Wendy, but she suspected Wendy was content to know that her best friend was special enough to entertain creatures from a fantasy realm.

The girls made their way to the huge oak tree and found Fiona and Ronan sitting there with an assortment of treats and snacks laid out on a small tree stump.

"I thought you'd never get here," Ronan complained, reaching for a colorful flower-shaped cookie. "I'm starving."

"Oh please, Ronan," Fiona said, "we're fairies. We don't really eat that much."

"Speak for yourself," he said, shoving the entire cookie into his mouth. Quite amazing since it was a human size cookie and he had a fairy size mouth.

"It's my fault we're late," Wendy admitted. "I was still cleaning my room."

Sarah Grace covered her mouth and giggled. "Ever since the adoption, you've been the perfect child. They can't give you away, you know. You belong to them."

"So, has Devon kissed you yet?" Wendy needled her friend.

"Could you possibly be any grosser?" Sarah Grace blurted out. "I'd sooner kiss a frog."

"Sarah Grace, you do know everyone at school was talking about you and him," Wendy giggled. "He likes you a lot."

As the munching and crunching and gluttony went on, Sarah Grace's mind drifted to a quiet song on the passing breeze. Grammy dying was the most devastating thing that ever happened to her. All the things the grieving are told, to make themselves feel better, were nothing but a bitter onslaught to her heart and mind the day of the funeral. She was in a deep and suffocating hole from which she thought she'd never escape, until she found the gem pouch among Grammy's things. At that moment she'd never felt more connected to her grandmother. She knew her grandmother was dancing across the breeze at this very moment, and one day, if Sarah Grace was lucky, she'd see her again in this life.

Fiona could tell what she was thinking. Cailins, she thought to herself. She still wasn't overly found of human children, but she had to admit there was something unique about Sarah Grace and Wendy. Sarah Grace had been successful because of her devotion to another child her age. Most fairies believed humans to be selfish and destructive. Fiona had been no different. Sarah Grace still had many lessons to learn and techniques to perfect. But, she already had the most important quality needed to succeed. **HEART**.

www.ingramcontent.com/pod-product-compliance
Lightning Source LLC
Chambersburg PA
CBHW032047240626
47154CB00003B/1107